DADDY BY DECEMBER

A DADDY IN THE MAKING...

A little girl, a wish, and a woman determined to stay out of his reach. How to reconcile the three?

Billionaire investor, Drake Duncan, is at the top of his game. He decides to hire a ghostwriter to work on his memoir. Little does he know that the writer who will answer the call is truly a ghost - from his past.

Meg Gracey is the proverbial 'starving artist', a writer down on her luck. When she is offered a contract as ghost- writer, she jumps at the chance, only to later realize that the job will throw her directly in the path of the man she'd vowed never to 'touch with a long stick'. Caught between starvation and emotional torture she is forced to choose.

Does she follow reason, or give in to the desires of her heart?

4

DADDY BY DECEMBER

JUDY ANGELO

The BILLIONAIRE BROTHERHOOD
Series
Volume 7

CHAPTER ONE

"**I** want her."

"But what about looking at the others?"

"No, this is the one I want." Drake Duncan stabbed the paper with his index finger. "I read through all the profiles. This one's the perfect fit. Professional, good track record. Got some novels under her belt, too. I don't want anyone who's so cast in the 'biography' mold that they don't know how to weave a good story."

His personal assistant gave him a look tinged with doubt. "I was going to recommend Percy Slater. He's worked with stars from Hollywood."

"Yeah, I've read some of his books. Boring."

Drake grinned at the gray-haired woman as she pursed her lips and gave him a disapproving stare. Liz Dobson had been working for him for the past eight years and she'd become more and more valuable to him with each passing year. No-one could anticipate his needs and organize his work life like she could. But in this matter, he would make the final decision.

"Fine," she said, with a nod of resignation. "I'll contact Ms. Gracey right away." She gathered up the files and went through the door, pulling it closed behind her.

Drake Duncan was looking for a ghostwriter. He was at the top of his game, leading a conglomerate of investment companies and, he decided, it was time to tell his story. After all, you never knew when your ticket would be called.

When he'd heard of the passing of Steve Jobs of Apple Computer, it had been like a kick to the gut. The man should have had a good thirty more years to go before he even thought of leaving this earth. But there it was. It was his time, and no amount of money could save him. Not that Drake was anywhere near Steve Jobs' age of fifty-six when he passed. But age had nothing to do with it. You could go at any time, so if you had a story to tell the best thing to do was just tell it.,

Drake had built Duncan Investments of Chicago into a billion-dollar company in the space of nine years through a series of daring but successful investment strategies. Even in the face of the worldwide economic recession, he was able to maximize growth for the corporation, making his shareholders wealthier than they'd ever dreamed. Now, he was ready to share his success with the world.

He smiled to himself. He was looking forward to the project. His ghostwriter would be Meg Gracey, if she accepted the job offer. He liked that name. Outside of the profile and recommendations she'd posted on the job board, he didn't know anything about the woman he'd chosen to record his journey. Liz would check her out.

He had a good feeling about her, though. Her name had the sound of someone dignified, someone serene. For the next few months, she would be spending a lot of time with him, gathering the intimate details of his business and his life. He hoped she did, indeed, have a serene soul. Working with him, she was going to need it.

MEG GRACEY PULLED UP in front of Hyde Park Elementary School just as the bell rang. Whew! Just in time.

She'd fought through a mangled mess of traffic, whispering prayers for the cars to get moving. Now, she breathed a sigh of relief. It was tough. being a single mommy. There was no-one to call, if she got held up at an appointment. She had to plan each day precisely, so she would never be late to pick up her daughter. This was Jessie's second semester in the first grade, and so far, thank God, she'd never been late.

She switched off the engine and hopped out of the car then ran along the pathway leading to the huge front door. At that moment, it burst open, and she had to head for the grass to avoid the bubbling mass of kids streaming down the steps toward their waiting parents. She stood on tiptoe, trying to find that special curly blonde head in the crowd.

"Mommy!"

She would know that voice anywhere, pluck it from the myriad of shouts and calls. She turned to catch the little bundle of pink and white barreling toward her. Jessie jumped and Meg lifted her into her arms, backpack, lunch kit and all. She hugged her daughter close and buried her nose in the child's neck, reveling in the tightness of her hug and the bubblegum scent of her hair. She gave her a quick peck on the forehead then gently lowered her to the ground and took her small, gloved hand.

"So, how was your day?" Meg asked, as she always did, her smile broad and cheerful.

"Mommy, guess what?" Jessie opened her blue eyes wide, a look of wonder on her pixie face. "I saw a bunny today; a real live bunny, not the Easter Bunny."

"A real live bunny, huh?" Meg took the lunch kit from her hand and they headed down the path toward the champagne colored Honda Accord. "That's really cool."

"Oh, yes." Jessie's voice was a soft whisper of reverence. "I got to touch him, and everything. He's so soft and cuddly.

Can I get one?"

Meg chuckled and shook her head. She'd expected that. Jessie loved animals, and seized every opportunity to put in her bid for a pet. Her goldfish, Sammy, was not enough. The big complaint? He wasn't cuddly. "You know why we can't get a pet right now, Jess. We talked about it, remember?" She opened the back door of the car and slid the Dora bag off her daughter's back.

Jessie gave a pretty pout as she climbed into her booster seat. "I know. Pets are a lot of responsibility, and I'm not old enough yet."

"That's right." Meg buckled her up then tickled her, making her squirm. "But when you're old enough..." Jessie giggled. "When I'm old enough, I can get a lemur and a tiger and a bear, and we'll start our own zoo."

Meg smiled at their ongoing joke. "And when Mommy lands the biggest writing contract ever, we'll add a giraffe and a pony."

"Yay." The little girl raised her hands in celebration and Meg laughed out loud. There was nothing like the enthusiasm of a child, to lift your spirits.

That afternoon, Meg and Jessie sang nursery rhymes and fun songs all the way home. Her daughter was such a bundle of joy. At five years old, she was the youngest in her first-grade class. The first day of elementary school had been hard for Meg, watching her baby, so tiny among the other children, leaving her to enter the building she called 'big kids' school'. Now that they were almost halfway through the school year, it had gotten a little bit easier for her to leave her daughter.

The singing was soothing therapy for Meg. She needed it, after the grueling day she'd had. Despite the cheery face she showed Jessie, inside, she was in turmoil. That morning, she'd done yet another job interview, this time for the position of technical writer with a law firm, but she knew the likelihood of her getting the job was slim. There had been seventeen other applicants vying for the same position, all of them placed in the same room to fill out the application form. It had been so demoralizing.

The life of a writer was not easy, particularly in an economic environment where it had become even harder to get picked up by agents and publishers.

Three years earlier, she'd given up her teaching career to pursue her life passion and she'd achieved some measure of success, selling seven of her contemporary romance manuscripts and making a reasonable living, enough to sustain herself and her daughter. But the past six months had been brutal. She had two manuscripts still sitting on editors' desks, and at the same time, she had bills to pay. With reality staring her in the face, she started putting out ads on craigslist.com and on job boards, offering her services as a ghostwriter. So far, the phone hadn't been ringing off the hook with calls from people wanting to write their memoirs or the novel of their hearts. The stupid phone hadn't rung once since she'd posted the ads.

Not one to roll over and die, she'd started looking for writing work in the technical field – brochures, product manuals, websites – but the market had lots of job hunters with tons of experience in that area. Why would anyone hire her over them? Still, she kept on trying. Tomorrow was another day. She would get up early and start the search all over again.

As they pulled into the underground parking garage, Meg pasted a practiced smile on her lips and turned to her daughter who sat humming in the back seat. She was sure Jessie would be a singer one day. Whenever she sang her sea-blue eyes sparkled, and she would shake her head till her sunshine curls bounced around her cheeks. She adored music.

"Ready to go, sweetie?"

"Can we have spaghetti for dinner?" Jessie gave her a cherubic smile as she began to unbuckle her seatbelt.

"Honey, we had spaghetti yesterday. And the day before. No more spaghetti." Meg wiggled her finger at the little gir,l but she just laughed.

Jessie knew she had her mother wrapped around her little finger and she used that knowledge to full advantage.

"Spaghetti, spaghetti, spaghetti," she chanted, then laughed out loud as Meg reached over to tickle her.

That evening, they came to a compromise. They didn't have spaghetti for dinner but they did have Jessie's next favorite dish – macaroni and cheese pie. Meg made sure she ate some baked chicken with it. The little girl would live on pasta alone, if she could. Then, that night as the bedside clock struck eight, they climbed into Jessie's twin bed, where she leaned against her mother and they read fairy tales until the eyelids drooped and the little head sagged. Then Meg slid slowly out of the bed, laid her daughter's head on the pillow, and pulled the blanket up under her chin. She leaned over and kissed the curly little head, then reached over and switched off the bedside lamp.

"G'night, Jessie," she whispered to her sleeping child, then slipped out the door.

Now that Jessie was down for the night, it was time for Meg to get down to her usual order of business – job hunting. The night before, she'd been at it into the wee hours of the morning, and tonight she was dead tired, but she did not have the luxury of taking even one night off. Her savings were dwindling. She had to find work, and fast.

Meg sat at the dining table and munched on an apple as she booted up her computer. She hadn't done her exercises today; hadn't gone on the stationary bike for the last four days, actually. She'd been so preoccupied, that she'd slipped up on the one thing she'd always told herself she would never compromise on. As far as she was concerned, exercise was the number one factor for good health, and with a daughter to take care of, she needed to stay healthy. Oh, well, at least she was getting in a serving of fruit before the day expired. An apple a day was better than nothing.

She'd been lost in thought for several seconds, before she realized that the computer screen was displaying the opening page of her e-mail account. She'd entered the password without even realizing it. She often did things on autopilot. Now, as she stared at the screen, she frowned. Was she seeing right? After weeks and weeks of advertising and posting, there, in her mailbox, was a reply entitled 'Ghostwriter for Hire'. Someone had responded to her ad.

Heart skipping in anticipation, she raised a hand that trembled slightly. She clicked on the mouse. The screen popped open, and she read the message. "We would like to meet with you regarding engaging your services as a ghostwriter. If we can agree on mutually acceptable terms..." She read on and the more she read, the more excited she got. Whoever it was, they wanted to hire her immediately. The words were like music to her heart.

They were based right there in Chicago, the story would be based on the experiences of the CEO of the corporation, and they wanted someone whose timing was flexible. Okay, that part might be a bit tricky but, somehow, she would get around it. She had a babysitter and a neighbor who watched Jessie every now and then. She might have to call on them for those times when this client might want her to be available on the weekend. Whatever it took, she would have to make it work.

Meg slumped back in the chair, relief flooding through her. She could finally see light at the bottom of the dismal hole into which she had fallen. She was grinning like an idiot, but she didn't care. She could do the happy dance right now and not feel a twinge of embarrassment. Unless, of course, the grumpy old super came to the door and found her doing the dance in her T-shirt-for-nightdress, bunny slippers and her head tied up in a red and white polka dot scarf.

Meg was still smiling as she reached for a pen and a sheet of paper to record the details of the company that had made the offer. And that was when she saw the name. She froze. Her mouth went slack. Duncan Investments. And the CEO was none other than Drake Duncan, the man who had broken her heart.

CHAPTER TWO

Meg gasped and slumped back in her chair, this time not in relief, but in shock. She could not believe it. The lifeline she'd been thrown had come from the very man she had tried so hard to forget. So many years had passed. She didn't even know if he would still remember her. But she remembered him, just as clearly as if they'd just met. There was no way in the world she would ever forget the man who had taken her virginity.

Biting her lip, Meg sucked in a deep breath, then got up from the table and walked over to the window. At the realization, her soaring heart had plummeted down to her toes. The disappointment was thick on her tongue, and she felt a warning prick behind her eyes. No, this was not the time for tears. She had to think.

She wanted the money. Badly. But how could she let Drake Duncan back into her life?

She remembered that fateful night like it was yesterday. She'd been twenty years old when she'd met the tall, suave and excruciatingly handsome senior in Philosophy 401. She'd been a junior then, shy and reserved, and had been taken aback when, at the end of year dance, Drake had ignored the girls fishing around him and had asked her for the last dance. It hadn't been in Meg's power to refuse. She'd been fantasizing about him all semester, knowing fully well that she had no hope of ever being with a man like that. He was the darling of the university, on the Dean's List, and a star on the swim team. Why would he even look at her?

But here he was, with his hand held out to her, inviting her to slow dance with him. She raised startled eyes to him and placed her trembling hand in his. Did he know she was madly in love with him? Could he feel her heart beating wildly in her chest? The thoughts chased one another around in her head, drowning out the music that pulsated in the auditorium. She shook her head, pushed her doubts to the back of her mind, and gave him a bright smile. Bravely, she stood up and stepped into his arms.

For Meg, the night was like something out of a fairy tale. She felt like Cinderella, not deserving the attention of the prince, but basking in the glory of it, just the same. She almost expected him to disappear at the stroke of midnight. But no such thing happened. In fact, at the end of the dance, he walked her all the way back to the dorm room she shared with her roommate. Thinking Amy was in, Meg opened the door, feeling safe in the expectation that his visit would be chaperoned. But there was no Amy there. She'd probably decided to spend the last night before graduation with her boyfriend.

Not wanting to look like an idiot, Meg invited him in, anyway. There were beers in the fridge, compliments of Amy, who was already twenty-one, so she offered him one. He accepted. And so, they sat and talked while Drake had a drink, and then another. He was relaxed, lounging in the sofa, while she perched on the edge of the armchair. By the time Meg offered Drake a third beer, she'd become just a bit more comfortable with him, charmed by his humor and worldly air. Who would have thought that Drake Duncan would choose to spend his last night before graduation talking to her?

Though they'd been in the same class of over a hundred students, he admitted that he'd only begun to notice her when she'd presented her paper to the class the week before. She giggled in embarrassment when he told her how he'd admired how professional she'd seemed as she addressed the class. Like a real philosopher, he said. She glowed with pride at his words. Drake Duncan admired her. But did he like her, too? Was that why he'd invited her to dance?

And then, he said them, the words she'd been dying to hear all night, all semester, all her life. "You're a beautiful girl, Meg. I don't know how I never noticed you before." He gave her a boyish grin. "I think I like you."

He patted the seat beside him. "Come sit over here. There's lots of space, and you sure don't look comfortable over there." When she hesitated, he gave her a gentle smile. "Come on, we'll just relax and watch some TV. I'm not going to bite."

Meg swallowed. "TV? But...it's kind of late..."

"Just for a little while. I want to see the replay of today's big game. It's more fun watching it with you than back in my room. Can't get too much football, right?"

He patted the seat again, and this time, Meg moved. He was right. What harm was there in watching some television with him? It was probably the last time she would see Drake Duncan before he graduated and headed off to another life, so it made sense to savor every moment with him. She got up off the chair and took the three steps to the sofa where he took her hand and pulled her down to sit beside him.

Drake was true to his word. He flipped channels until he found the game, and they watched play after play, comfortable in each other's company. Eventually, though, the late hour got the best of Meg, and her eyelids began to droop. She was barely aware of her head sliding to rest against Drake's warm shoulder, and then she was gone.

When Meg woke up, she found herself lying on Drake's chest, her head tucked under his chin. He was sprawled in the sofa, his chest rising and falling gently, his heart beating in a slow and steady rhythm. He was fast asleep. Slowly, she lifted her head, and in the soft glow from the TV, she got her first really close look at the man of her dreams. She still could not believe that she was lying in his arms. Could this be a dream? Was she asleep and just fantasizing again? Well, if it was all a dream, then she might as well make use of it. She might never get the chance again.

Gently, so as not to wake him, Meg slid up Drake's body until her face was over his. She smiled down at him. He looked so peaceful, so innocent when he slept. Gone were the crooked grin and the slight cock of the eyebrows. This was the real Drake Duncan, and she was probably the only girl in the whole school who had seen him this way. Suddenly, she was no longer afraid of him. She no longer saw him as a young god on earth. He was lying right there beneath her, big and warm, a man of flesh and blood. And she wanted him. Gosh, did she ever want him.

With a sudden surge of adrenalin, came a bravery which made Meg lose her usual shyness and do something she would not normally have dared. Before she could change her mind, she closed her eyes and pressed her lips to Drake's, savoring the feel of his mouth against hers. When he moaned, still deep in sleep, she slid her arm up around his neck and pressed her body into his, totally aroused by his groan. He was moaning for her, only for her, and the thought made her nipples peak inside her bra. She kissed him harder.

And then, he was kissing her back. She had no idea at what point he came to consciousness, but before she knew what was happening, she was no longer in control. He had his hand at her back now, anchoring her body to his, while his other hand slid up to cup her head and angle her face so that he had full access to her lips. He was kissing her, all the desire she was feeling reflected in the passion of his kiss.

"Mmm, Meg," he breathed, and then he rolled over until he was the one lying on top, even as he continued to kiss her senseless. He slid his mouth from hers and then, with his lips, he was tickling the skin of her cheek, her neck, her collarbone, until his fingers pushed away the lace of her bra, and he was nuzzling her breast.

When he sucked the nipple deep inside his mouth, Meg felt she would swoon from the sensation. Never had she been touched there by a man. And now his lips, his tongue, his teeth were on her, tickling and teasing, playing with her body until she arched her back, wanting even more of the sweet sensation.

"Meg, I want you so much," he murmured.

And she knew he did. He wanted her as much as she wanted him. His desire was plain in the hardness that pressed against her leg. Her desire was obvious in the heaving of her chest and her breathless panting. They both wanted it.

Meg shook her head, dragging herself out of her reverie and back to the present. No, she did not want to revisit that night. Not now. Not when she had a serious decision to make. It had been beautiful, that was true. As he reached for his wallet Drake had hesitated, wanting to know if she was sure, but she'd been eager, wanting it more than anything in the world. And he'd been gentle, oh so gentle, almost as if he'd known it was her first time. He'd been perfect, taking her to heights she had never climbed before.

But it was what happened afterward that made her cringe. After the act, she'd been overcome with feelings of guilt and shame. This had been their first date, if you could call it that, and what had she done? She'd gone and slept with him. What must he think of her? She couldn't bear to look him in the face. What if, for him, this was just a one-night stand?

DADDY BY DECEMBER 11

And what else could it be, anyway? He would be leaving the university the next day and, chances were, she would never see him again. She couldn't bear to think about it.

After that, she'd been very quiet, drawing into her shell. He'd seemed confused at the change in her. He tried to speak to her, but she shook her head, the tears at the point of spilling over. But she held on till he'd gone through the door, and then she'd closed it. Only then did she let the torrent of tears burst free.

If he called her next day, then she would know he had true feelings for her. But what if he didn't? And why should he? He'd gotten what he wanted. Wasn't that how college guys were? Once they'd had a taste, they lost all interest in you and moved on to the next conquest. And that was all she was, just a conquest. Why else would a jock like Drake have paid any attention to her?

And, just as she anticipated, she never heard from Drake Duncan again. Graduation day came and she was in the crowd when he walked up to receive his diploma. With honors, of course. Then, she'd gone back to her room and waited. And waited. And waited until the sun went down behind the hills and her roommate yawned her goodnight.

That night, Meg did not sleep at all. She was packing all through the night, and first thing in the morning she was heading for the bus station. She would not put herself through any more torture. She had accepted her fate. She'd suffered the fate of so many other college girls before her, and she'd learned a lesson she would never forget.

Now, that lesson had come back to haunt her in a very real way. If she was not careful, Drake Duncan would be back in her life and back in her heart. Of course, she'd known how big he had become in Chicago. His rise in fortune had been phenomenal and he was often featured in Illinois newspapers. But she'd vowed she would never make herself known to him, never attempt to even go near him. But fight as she would, it seemed that fate had other plans. The gods had thrown him in her path and, as it was before, it was her decision. And this time, she had to make it the right one.

"COME ON, JESSIE. GRAB your lunch kit. I have your school bag."

"Coming, Mommy." Jessie came racing into the living room, her pink woolly hat in one hand and her hand-knitted gloves in the other. "I just wanted to kiss Miss Kitty goodbye."

Meg gave her daughter a warm smile and bundled her into her jacket. Jessie never left the house without saying goodbye to her favorite toy. Miss Kitty had been a gift from her grandmother for her second birthday and she loved her just as much now as she had when she just got it. When other kids clung to a beloved 'blankie', Jessie clung to Miss Kitty.

"Okay, let's go." Meg grabbed Jessie's backpack and her handbag with one hand and took her daughter's hand with the other. As the little girl chattered away, they went out the door and down the driveway to the car.

As Meg drove her daughter to school, her mind drifted away from the conversation. She gave her usual responses of 'Yes, sweetie" and "Of course, honey", but her mind was on what the rest of the day would bring. She'd stayed up late two nights before, thinking through her options, battling with the decision until, finally, she had come to the conclusion that she needed to accept the contract.

It would be difficult for her, that was for sure, but the man was offering five figures to get his memoir written. And it was not as if there were any other offers on the table. She had the rent to pay and her daughter to feed and clothe. She would just have to bear things for the months that it would take to get the job done. Then, she would bury him once more in the back of her mind and get on with her life.

And so, the next day she'd called and made an appointment to see him that very week - before she had a chance to change her mind.

The main office of Duncan Investments was impressive. Meg pulled into the parking lot, then walked up the driveway to the twenty-story building fashioned in black tinted glass and silver beams. It had a futuristic look and feel that made her wonder at the man Drake Duncan had become. From his days at the university, he'd been voted as most likely to succeed. He'd been touted as a progressive and innovative thinker. And look where it had taken him. She was not surprised.

Meg signed in at the security desk and rode the glass paneled elevator up to the top floor. There, she checked in at the receptionist's desk.

"Please have a seat, Ms. Gracey," the smiling young woman told her. Mr. Duncan will see you in just a few minutes."

Meg sank gratefully into the plush leather sofa in the waiting lounge. She felt like her knees were turning to Jello so, she was glad for an excuse to get off her feet. Then, she slid forward and perched on the edge with her handbag propped on her knees. Her palms were moist, and with each passing moment there was a quickening in the rhythm of her beating heart. Goodness, it was sheer torture, sitting there, anticipating their meeting.

"Ms. Gracey?"

At the sound of her name, Meg jumped. She looked up and found herself staring into the warm brown eyes of a gray- haired woman in a navy-blue suit.

"Yes," Meg said with a nod, and hopped up off the seat.

"My name is Liz Dobson. I'm Mr. Duncan's personal assistant." The woman held out her hand and gave Meg a firm handshake. "Thanks for making yourself available so quickly. I'll take you to see Mr. Duncan now." As if sensing her vis,itor's nervousness the woman smiled at her again, then turned toward the heavy oak door that led to the inner offices.

Meg followed, feeling like a lamb being led to the slaughter, but she sucked in her breath, straightened her back and put on her bravest face. Even if she melted inside, Drake Duncan must never know.

They walked down a long passage until finally they came to another oak door. Liz gave a gentle tap then pushed it open and stood aside, indicating with a nod that Meg should go in. She nodded and stepped past the woman and onto the plush cream carpet of Drake Duncan's private office.

And there he was, sitting in the high-backed leather chair, the phone receiver to his left ear, a gold pen in his right hand, as he scribbled on a yellow notepad. He looked worldly, powerful, and even more handsome than she remembered. Gone, were the hooded sweatshirt and jeans of his campus days. Those had been replaced with a charcoal-gray suit, white button-down shirt and wine-colored tie. His hair was different, too. Instead of the crew cut of his youth, his hair now coiled at the nape of his neck, giving him the look of a sexy male model rather than a billionaire businessman. All this, Meg saw in a split second.

And yet, he was not looking at her.

And then suddenly, he was.

As he reached over to hang up the phone, he lifted his head, and a smile softened his firm lips. "I'm sorry. Just had to finish a quick call." He got up from behind his desk and she was reminded of how tall he was. At well over six feet, he towered over both of the women in the office. He walked over, his hand outstretched.

"Thank you for coming, Miss Gracey," he said, as he took her hand in a strong grip. "Glad you accepted my offer."

"Mrs. Gracey," she corrected, and lifted her head to look straight into his striking gray eyes.

Drake Duncan froze. His grip on her hand tightened and his brows furrowed. "Meg...Donovan?"

Her heart leaped and, to her chagrin, she felt a slight trembling in her lip. She bit down on it.

He had remembered. After all these years, he still recognized the pathetic little junior who had thrown herself at him. She didn't know whether to feel elated or dismayed. What she felt, was nervous. Would he reject her because of their past encounter?

For the moment, Meg could not speak. All she could do was nod.

Shock registered on his face. His brows raised and he sucked in a quick breath. There was an expression on his face that she could not read.

Oh, Lord. What had she done? In coming here. had she just made the second biggest mistake of her life?

DADDY BY DECEMBER 13

DRAKE DUNCAN COULD not tear his eyes away.

Meg Donovan. She was here, standing right in front of him, looking even more beautiful than when he had last held her in his arms. And his body remembered her. Even before she'd lifted her face to his, before he'd had a good look at her, he'd known. The moment his hand touched hers, an electric charge ran through him, so strong, that he'd held her tight. It was either that or whip his hand away from the shock.

Meg, in living color, all five feet five inches of her. Where she used to have wild, chestnut curls framing her pixie face, her hair was now swept up in a sleek ponytail that flowed, long and straight, down her back. Her hazel eyes were huge in her face and her lips, those full, soft lips he remembered, now trembled under his gaze. Everything around him disappeared and all he could see was that sweet, innocent girl he had fallen for, so many years ago.

Get a grip, Drake. That was another lifetime. And she walked away, remember?

In the microsecond it took for Drake to take things in, he realized he was still holding her hand. He released her and shoved his tingling hand deep in his pocket. But still, he did not look away.

Liz cleared her throat. "May I get you anything, Ms. Gracey? Coffee? Tea?"

It took that interruption for the spell to be broken. Drake stepped away and went to pull out the chair in front of his desk. He pasted a smile on his face and nodded to Meg. "Please, have a seat."

Hesitantly, she took a step toward him. Then she paused and looked at Liz. "A cup of tea would be nice," she said, smiling at the woman. "Thank you." Then she took the two steps to the chair and gracefully sank down into it.

Drake released the back of Meg's chair and walked around his desk. He took his time getting there. He needed those two seconds to gather his thoughts. Meg had hurtled back into his life, slamming him back against the wall of a reality he thought he'd buried years ago. He'd wanted Meg Donovan from the day he'd seen her at the podium, so small and yet so brave, speaking to a lecture hall of over a hundred of her peers. He'd wanted her even more when they danced at the pre-graduation party. And, after having one taste of her that night, he'd wanted her for life.

And, to his chagrin, none of that had changed. Seeing her again, holding her hand in his, had the feelings barreling into him as if not a day had passed. He wanted this woman just as much as he had, from day one. But now, there was a problem. A major one. Meg Donovan was married.

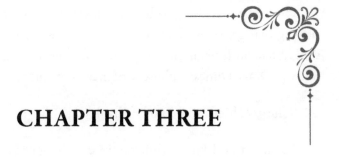

CHAPTER THREE

As Drake walked back to his chair, Meg folded her hands in her lap and held her breath. Gracious, what had she gotten herself into? As she stared at his broad back, her mouth went dry, and she knew she hadn't lost the attraction she'd felt for him. Oh Lord, she was in trouble.

Drake sat down and rested his crossed arms on the desk. "Thank you for coming," he said, his voice deep and low and so sexy that she felt a blush creep up her neck. "Under the circumstances, you didn't have to, so I appreciate it."

That brought her back to earth with a bump. 'Under the circumstances' he'd said. Meaning what? I used you, then dumped you, so I didn't expect you to show up at my office? Was he rubbing it in? A wave of humiliation washed over her, and her palms went damp. If she didn't need the money so desperately, she would get up and walk right out. But sadly, she did. She had to put her feelings aside and think of Jessie. She drew in a breath and let it out slowly, willing herself to stay calm.

Then she looked up and caught him staring at her with hooded eyes that made it impossible for her to read his expression. As her eyes darted up to his, he blinked, then cleared his throat.

"You have an impressive profile, Meg," he began, then said quickly, "I mean, Mrs. Gracey."

Oh, so he was going to be formal, was he? She was very good at playing that game. And anyway, maybe it was for the best that they should remain formal. That way, she would never forget her position. She was Drake Duncan's ghost- writer, nothing more.

She gave him a slight nod. "Thank you."

"Even before I knew who you were, I thought you would be the perfect person to write my memoir." His face became more animated, as if he was beginning to relax in her presence. "So many novels under your belt, one of them on the USA Today Best Seller List."

She couldn't help smiling at that one. "Oh, so you've been reading up on me."

"Of course," he said, with a smile that brought a twinkle to his eyes, and for a moment, he looked just like the Drake Duncan she'd swooned over in college. The years fell away, and the person she saw before her was the tall, muscled athlete that all the girls chased after.

Except that he was even more handsome now than he'd been ten years ago. There was a worldliness about him, a self-confidence and sophistication that hadn't been there before. If he'd been a lady killer then, she could just imagine what he was now, successful and super handsome and single. Yes, he was still single. He'd read up on her. but she'd read up on him, too. And she knew he was one of the wealthiest eligible bachelors in Chicago.

But that meant nothing to her. She was here to do a job, and she would do it to the best of her ability and then be on her way.

"I guess the project will take anywhere from three to six months," he was saying, "but you're the writer. You know best. I'm relying on you to work out an appropriate schedule."

"No problem," she said, her tone brisk. "Before I start writing anything I'll have to do a series of detailed interviews then I'll compile my notes and get started." She pointed to the desk calendar. "If you just hand that to me, I can set up the interview dates right now."

He slid it over to her, and this time she made sure their hands didn't touch. That would be too much to handle. Right then, all she wanted to do was deal with the business at hand and then get the heck out of that office. In that space, she was too close to Drake for comfort.

He looked at the dates she'd highlighted. "So, we start next week?" She nodded. "Monday afternoon, before the week gets on the way."

"What about this week?" he asked. "I want to get started as soon as possible."

14

---❦---

DADDY BY DECEMBER 15

She shook her head. "No can do. I need this week to arrange my business so that once I get started, I can just focus.

I NEED TO ARRANGE FOR a babysitter for those days when I need to be here."

"You...have children?" A stricken look crossed his face, then in a flash, it was gone.

Meg frowned. So, what if she had children? Would that be an issue? It certainly wouldn't affect the quality of her work. "I have a five-year-old," she said, her tone slightly defensive. "My daughter, Jessie."

"Oh," he said. "That's...nice."

His words were appropriate, but Meg could see that her having a child had affected him in some way. His face had gone still and his voice quiet. Now, he seemed to be deep in thought.

"Is that a problem?"

His eyes snapped back to her face. "Excuse me?"

"Is it a problem that I have a child? You don't seem too happy about it."

"No, not at all." He had the grace to look ashamed. "I guess I'm just getting used to the idea of you having a family." Meg almost laughed. It had been ten years since she'd last seen or spoken to this man. Did he expect her to believe

that she'd actually crossed his mind even once over those ten years?

On the other hand, he'd crossed her mind a lot. She couldn't count the number of nights she'd cried herself to sleep, thinking about Drake and how he'd stolen her heart, only to then turn around and stomp it into the dust. And now, he had the audacity to pretend as if he'd spent any time thinking about her. As she thought about it she felt the anger build inside.

She glared at him. "Well, I'm glad my daughter is not a concern for you. I assure you, my dealings with you will be quite professional, so you have no need to worry about Jessie getting in the way of your project."

He frowned, seeming perturbed. "I wasn't thinking that at all," he said, his tone leaving her in no doubt that he was annoyed. "I have no question about your professionalism, Mrs. Gracey. I know you're the best."

There he went again, addressing her in that formal tone. And, to her chagrin, instead of feeling triumphant, she only felt depressed. *Get a grip, Meg. You're far too emotional today.*

He stood up, his brow furrowed, his face cloudy with an emotion that looked like a cross between anger and pain. "I'm sure you're not only a great writer but an excellent mother as well." He shoved his fists deep into his pocket. "Your husband is a lucky man."

Meg's breath caught in her throat. She bit her lip and looked away. "Was," she whispered, the word almost choking
her.

Drake was turning away, when he froze. She could see him from the corner of her eye.

"Was?" His voice was hoarse, almost harsh. Slowly, he turned and looked down at her, his gray eyes like molten steel. "Are you divorced?"

Meg drew in a deep breath, and for a few seconds, she said nothing. Then, she exhaled and shook her head. "I almost wish that was it." Her voice came out quiet and calm, so different from how she really felt. "My husband is dead." She lifted her eyes then, and she could see that her words had shocked him into silence. Eyebrows raised, he looked almost unbelieving, but then he let out his breath and his face turned somber, as if he was genuinely sympathetic to her loss. "I'm very sorry to hear this. I had no idea."

She gave a dry, mirthless laugh. "I didn't expect you to. After all, you know nothing about me. We haven't seen each other in over ten years."

The instant the words left her mouth, Meg regretted it. She sounded absolutely pathetic. Now, what if the man thought she'd been pining for him? She tightened her lips and glared up at him. He'd better not think, that because it wasn't true.

But when she looked up at him, there was not a hint of gloating on his face. Instead, his expression was one of concern, even pity. It was clear that he'd been moved by her news.

16 JUDY ANGELO

"Sorry," she said, wishing she could take back the rash words that had tumbled out of her mouth. As far as she was concerned, she'd made a poor impression on her first meeting with Drake. The best thing she could do right then was leave. She would regroup and come back another day, fresh and strong.

She got up and held out her hand to Drake. "Thank you for choosing me for your project," she said. "I'll do my best to give you a memoir worthy of your name."

He nodded and took her hand in his. "I look forward to it," he said softly.

They exchanged polite smiles, the smiles of strangers, and then he walked her to the door.

"GO, HORSEY, GO."

Drake groaned under the harsh treatment of his diminutive jockey. He was on all fours, his three-year-old nephew straddling his back with his chubby legs, and he was being whipped soundly with a long ruler.

"Faster, horsey, faster." The little boy bounced up and down on his uncle's back but that only made the horsey slow from an already lumbering pace to almost a complete stop.

"Unca," the boy wailed, "I want horsey to move." He grabbed the collar of his uncle's shirt and jerked back and forth.

The horse didn't even budge. Frustrated, he opened his mouth wide and yelled, "Mommy, Unca's not playin' nice." "Horsey," came the female voice from the kitchen, "what are you out there doing to my boy?"

Drake gave a soft chuckle. "Not a thing," he said. "Horsey's just tired. He's not as young as he used to be."

The truth was, today Drake was too distracted to focus all his attention on little Andrew. The boy had been riding him for the last twenty minutes and normally he would've been rearing up on hind legs, forcing Andy to cling on for dear life as he burst into peals of laughter, but today all he'd done was take him on a rather boring journey from the sofa to the fireplace to the front door and back again. Right now, Andrew was none too pleased at his horsey that had suddenly grown super old and cranky. But Drake couldn't help it. Meg Donovan – no, Gracey – had been on his mind since they'd shaken hands and she'd walked out of his office.

First, he'd been devastated to find out that she was married. Then he'd felt guilty that, married or not, he wanted her so bad he could almost taste her. And then, she told him her husband was dead. And what had he felt then? Swine that he was, his first reaction had been relief. Even before he'd felt sympathy for her loss, his heart had leaped inside his chest at the thought that he actually had a chance. How could he be so callous?

But on the other hand, how could he help it? Like a miracle, the woman he'd fallen for ten years ago had walked into his office and back into his life. Just like that. And just like that, his senses had gone haywire all over again. Shoot, he'd been twenty-three then, and yet, at his ripe old age of thirty-three, he was still bowled over by the sheer beauty of her.

Ten years ago, she'd been a shy junior, but now, she was a sophisticated woman - independent, competent and talented. How many writers could say they'd hit a best seller list? And, although under sad circumstances, she was available. At least, he thought she was. His mood grew serious as he thought about it. He really hoped she was.

"Andy, horsey needs to get some water, okay?" Drake looked over his shoulder at the now pouting Andrew. "Let's take a break."

"Aaw." Andrew didn't hide his disappointment, pouting even more, and folding his arms across his little chest. Drake could see his reflection in the plate glass window. His face turned stubborn, and Drake knew what that meant. He would have a fight getting him off his back.

"Now come on, Andrew. Slide off." Drake sat back on his haunches, but the boy wrapped his stout arms around his uncle's neck and refused to let go. Drake ended up having to pry his arms loose to get him to slide down to the floor. That set off a round of wailing that could be heard a mile away. Andrew ran off to his mother, finally leaving Drake in peace.

Now alone, his mind was free to wander back to that night he would never forget.

He'd been a senior, just a day away from graduation, when he'd finally struck up the courage to ask Meg Donovan to the graduation dance. He'd been admiring her for weeks but somehow, he'd felt hesitant. She seemed so innocent, yet so...aloof. She was like an exotic flower in a garden of daisies. How could anyone dare pluck a flower like that? Still, he'd asked her out and, lucky son-of-a-gun that he was, she'd accepted. They'd danced into the wee hours of the morning and then, unwilling to let the night end, he'd walked her back to her dorm room. He was surprised and grateful when she'd invited him in, but he'd tried his darnedest to be a gentleman, hiding the bulge in his pants and playing all casual and cool like there was nothing amiss.

He did a pretty good job of it. For a while. The trouble started when he drifted off and woke up to find the angel in his arms. She was lying on top of him and, dazed as he was, there was no way he could resist. Well, that was what he told himself. He'd wanted her so badly, he just didn't want to fight it.

And so, when she'd kissed him, he'd kissed back, and then he'd kept going, tasting her and caressing her, savoring her sweetness until he wanted nothing else but to possess her fully.

And she'd been so willing, so eager. What sane man would have said no?

They made sweet music that night, and when he found out this would be her first time, he'd been gentle, coaxing her and bringing her to her peak of ecstasy. She'd cried out and his heart had swelled with love at the sound of his name on her lips. Strangely, though, after that, she'd been very quiet, but he'd put it down to the fact that this was all so new to her.

Drake's heart pounded as he recalled what happened next. He'd gone to meet his family for an early graduation breakfast celebration then, before he knew it, it was time to head off to the graduation. He'd had to rush to make it for the procession. After the ceremony, his college buddies whisked him off to yet another celebration, and then another, only releasing him in the wee hours just before the sun came up. Exhausted, he'd crashed on top of the bed and had not budged again until the sun was high in the sky.

Immediately, he thought of Meg, and feeling lightheaded and eager, he showered and dressed and hurried to her dorm room. But when he got there, she was gone.

"Where is she?" he practically shouted at her sleepy-looking roommate. "Already left," she said with a shrug.

"Left? For where?" he demanded, a sinking feeling creeping up inside him.

"Went home," the roommate said, with another shrug. "And if you're the guy she went dancing with last night, she never wants to see you again."

"What?" Drake could not believe his ears.

The roommate finally seemed to be waking up. She straightened and now she was glaring at him. "For your information, she said the guy took her dancing, but then he showed his true colors, and she didn't want to have anything to do with him again. Wouldn't touch him with a long stick." The girl had a smug expression on her face, almost as if she was enjoying being the bearer of bad news.

Drake stared back at her, confused. Showed his true colors? What the hell did that mean? And she never wanted to see him again? Just like that, she had thrown him out of her life?

Dazed, he turned away from the door. Was that all he'd been to her? One night of pleasure and that was it? But she'd been a virgin, for God's sake. Virgins didn't do one-night stands, did they?

Confused, deflated and defeated he dragged his way back to his dorm room. She wouldn't touch him with a long stick. That was what she'd said. Well, she wouldn't need that stick. He got the point. He would stay out of her way and out of her life.

And so, he had. He'd moved on with his life, gone through relationship after relationship, but he'd never again found that magical moment he'd shared with Meg Donovan. In vain, he'd kept looking, losing hope that he would ever again find that special connection – until now.

Meg Donovan was back in his life, and this time, he would not let her escape.

CHAPTER FOUR

"Oh, no." Meg put her finger to her mouth and began to nibble her nails. She was in big trouble.

There she'd gone, making that big speech about being professional and her child not getting in the way, and then today, on her way to her second interview with Drake, she'd received a call from the babysitter – she was down with the flu and couldn't help her out.

Meg almost groaned again but she glanced in the rear-view mirror and saw that Jessie was busy lecturing her dolly. "No more cookies for you," she said as firmly as a tiny girl's voice could go. "They'll give you cavities."

Meg couldn't help smiling, but then her thoughts went back to her dilemma. What was she going to do with Jessie?

She'd been on her way to the babysitter's house when she got the call. What was she going to do now?

All the people she could think of were already at work and her parents were too far away for her to just drop by. Meg sighed and put on her indicator then pulled over to the side of the road. There was only one thing to do – call and cancel her meeting.

She dialed the direct number Drake had given her and he picked up immediately.

"I'm so sorry," she said. "I won't be able to make our appointment today."

"What happened? Is everything all right?" To her relief, he sounded more concerned than angry.

"It's okay. Nothing happened. It's just..." She bit her lip. Should she tell him? It took her only a second to answer her own question. She had to be honest. "Jessie's babysitter cancelled on me just as I was on my way to drop her off. I can't find anyone else, not at such short notice. She's in the car with me right now."

"Why don't you take her with you? I can give her some paper and pencils. Maybe she can entertain herself for a while, so we can work."

Meg frowned. Was Drake Duncan going out of his way to be nice to her? "Are you sure? I don't want to turn your office into a mini daycare-"

"Meg," he said, cutting her off, "bring the child."

At that, Meg's brow knitted tighter. She hadn't expected this from him, but it certainly solved her immediate problem. "Well, if you think it's okay..."

"It is," he said, without hesitation. "Now, drive safely."

When he hung up, Meg rested her head on the steering wheel and gave a sigh of relief. Thank goodness, he was an understanding man. He may have been a jerk, but at least he had this one redeeming quality. He was sympathetic to the plight – and the scarcity of options – of a single mom.

Within fifteen minutes of their conversation, Meg was holding Jessie's hand as she rode the elevator up to the fortieth floor of the

Duncan Investments building. Eyes big as baby moons, Jessie watched
the numbers light up as they went higher and higher.

"Are we going all the way to the rooftop, Mommy?" she asked,
as she clung just a little bit tighter to her hand. She sidled closer and
pressed against her mother's hip.

Meg chuckled. "Almost. We're going to the penthouse floor." She
tousled her daughter's hair. "Don't worry. We're almost there."

She nodded her curly blonde head, but the way she clung to her
dolly, told Meg she still wasn't comfortable. When the elevator door
opened, she popped out even before her mother could take a step.

"I got out first. I beat you, Mommy."
"Yes, you did. You're the winner."

Before Jessie could give her usual celebratory yell, Meg caught up
with her and put a finger to her lips. "Now, we're going to be really
quiet when we go into the office, aren't we? Quiet as a mouse. Can we
do that?"

19

20 JUDY ANGELO

Jessie lifted her little shoulders then nodded. "Yes, Mommy,"
she said, in a staged whisper. "Quiet as a mouse."

The receptionist greeted them warmly and took them to Drake's
office. Jessie, eyes huge with wonder at the strange new sights, stopped
in the middle of the doorway and refused to take another step.

"Come on, Jessie." Meg took her hand and tried to urge her
forward, but she would not budge.

"So, is this the little princess who's come to entertain me?"

Meg looked up and there was Drake, all smiles, looking for all the world like a doting dad smiling down at his beloved daughter. There was not an ounce of guile about him. His smile looked genuine, and she found herself smiling back, grateful that he was making the effort to put her child at ease.

Jessie stepped closer to her mother as she stared shyly at Drake. "I'm not a princess," she said. "I'm a little girl." Drake paused and cocked his head to one side. "Are you sure you're not a princess?"

Jessie shook her head.

"Well, you look like a princess to me," Drake said, then he crouched down so the little girl could look him in the eyes. "And do you know what little princesses get?"

Her eyes big and blue, Jessie shook her head again.

"Candy canes." He got up and reached out to pluck a candy cane from the jar on the reception counter. Immediately, Jessie was all smiles. Gone were the shyness and the hesitation. She looked like the tension was beginning to leave her.

Meg shook her head. "I'm not sure candy is a good idea," she said, smiling. "Now she's going to stick to you like glue."

"I don't mind," he said, looking totally unconcerned. "My nephew is only three, so I'm used to having a little one around."

Meg watched as he took Jessie's hand and led her into hisS office and over to a small table on which were laid out several sheets of paper and colored pencils. He lifted the child onto the seat then stepped back. "There you go. An art studio of your own. Now, let me see what you can create."

It was so weird, watching this mega-powerful business executive, a billionaire no less, catering to the needs of her child. Who would have thought he would be so caring, so thoughtful as to go out of his way to make Jessie feel comfortable? This was the total opposite of how she'd seen him.

Could she have been wrong about him? He was nice now, but...no, she didn't think so. He was probably super nice to kids, but when it came to women, that was a whole other story. But she wouldn't let that concern her now. She had work to do.

While Jessie drew flowers and turtles and princesses in castles, Meg and Drake tackled the first phase of the project. Through a list of interview questions designed to elicit the key elements of Drake's story, she was able to record the first pages in his journey toward domination of the investment arena. For Meg it was a real eye-opener.

She learned that Drake hadn't started out poor. He was from a wealthy family, with generations of experience in investing and creating wealth. As a child, he'd picked up tips and investment strategies right there at the family dinner table. But once he left college and started his own business, his fortunes galloped past anything he or his family had ever dreamed of. He'd made a series of smart moves, which placed him solidly in the category of billionaire.

After about an hour of it, Meg went over to check on Jessie. "Are you okay, sweetie? Do you need anything?"

Jessie shrugged then shook her head, seeming totally absorbed in her current masterpiece, a drawing of a woman, a little girl and a man. He was tall, and she'd colored his hair yellow. He was holding the woman's hand. For a moment, Meg stared at the picture, almost afraid to ask. But then, in the end, she didn't have to.

"This is the daddy I want," Jessie said, in a voice as clear as crystal. If Meg had wanted to be discreet about the drawing, those hopes were dashed immediately. Jessie pointed to the stick figure of the man.

"Mommy, when are you going to get me a daddy? Can I get one for Christmas?"

DADDY BY DECEMBER 21

Meg's eyes widened and she had to fight not to slap her hand over Jessie's mouth. It was a conversation they'd had many times, but why here, why now? *Oh, Jessie, please. Not when Drake Duncan is hearing every word.*

"Uhm, we'll talk about that another time, Jess. You must be thirsty. Let's run downstairs and get your lunch kit." Meg started to bustle the child out of the chair but she pulled away.

"No, I want to finish my picture." Jessie's tone was adamant, which meant she wasn't planning on moving any time soon. Not without a fight.

"There's a cafeteria on the first floor." Drake's voice broke into their mini-struggle. He was standing there, watching them, the slight curl of his lips making his amusement obvious. "And some snacks in the conference room you just walked past. You would know what she likes. You can swing by there and choose her some juice and a snack; anything you think she would like.."

"Oh," she said, wondering why he was being so helpful. "Thank you. Come on, Jessie."

"No, Mommy, I want to stay. Can I stay, please?" Jessie turned on her whining voice and screwed up her face as if she was close to tears.

Meg knew that strategy well, one that Jessie used to garner the sympathy of onlookers. The little girl was a master at getting others on her side, then they'd all gang up on Meg to get her to give in to her daughter's wishes.

"Why don't you let her stay? She looks like she really wants to finish her picture."

Meg stared at Drake. Good heavens. Jessie's trick had worked on him, too. Defeated, she shook her head and walked to the door. "I'm sure she's hungry," she said. "I'll go get her something, if you don't mind."

Drake nodded. "Not at all. Go get her what she needs. Please."

Meg gave him a grateful smile. "It'll be quicker if I just go grab the stuff myself. Be back in a minute," she said, glancing at her child, whose attention was back on her drawing.

She looked totally absorbed. Guessing that she wouldn't be too much of a distraction for Drake, Meg went out the door.

And as she hurried down the hallway toward the conference room, she breathed a prayer that, while she was gone, Jessie would not, under any circumstances, mention a word about her wish for a daddy. As it was, Drake Duncan had already heard too much.

AS SOON AS HER MOTHER had walked out the door, Jessie laid her pencil down and turned guileless blue eyes up at Drake. "Can you help me?"

Drake gave her a small smile, trying to put her at ease. He reached out and pulled out one of the tiny chairs then, feeling like a giant, he sat down across from her.

"Is something the matter?" he asked, gently. "I'll do my best to help."

"Can you help me find a daddy by December twenty-four?"

Drake's eyebrows shot up, and then he shook his head. But, not wanting to scare the child, he tempered his reaction with a smile. "What do you mean, Jessie? Why do you need a daddy by that date?"

"It's for my mommy," she said, her little face earnest, as she stared up at him. "She never gets flowers for her birthday, or for Christmas, like my best friend's mom does, and she never, ever, gets roses for Valentine's Day. Sometimes she looks so sad..." Her voice trailed off and her face grew pensive. "I think if we had a daddy at our house like my friends do, then she would be happy." She turned her eyes back to him. "Can you help me find one?"

"Well, I'm..." He clamped his mouth shut. What the hell could he say to the kid? I'd love to apply for the position, but your mom would never have me? He cleared his throat as he tried to buy himself some time. "What's so special about December twenty-four?"

Jessie gave a tinkling laugh. "It's Christmas Eve, silly. That's the last day to tell Santa what presents you want." She leaned toward Drake then whispered, "I made Mommy think I want a daddy for me, but it's really for her. I want it to be a surprise."

Drake sat back in his little chair and stared across at the five-year-old matchmaker in admiration. Who would have known that such a tiny child would have the gray matter to plan to trick her mother into a relationship?

He shook his head slowly, as he contemplated Jessie. She was an observant little tyke, too, to notice her mother's lack of presents on those special days. Poor kid. It must have been hard for her, losing her daddy.

"You miss your daddy a lot, I guess," he said softly, not wanting to upset her with sad memories.

"Unh-unh." She shook her head vigorously.

Drake cocked his head to one side. "You don't?"

"I don't know my daddy," she said. "I mean, not anymore. I was too little when he died. Mommy said he was hit by a drunk driver."

Oh, shit. He didn't say it out loud. What a crappy way to die. The poor guy had probably been on his way home to his family when some idiot put out his lights forever. "I'm so sorry to hear-"

"I'm back."

Meg burst into the room, an overly bright smile on her face. "I got your juice." She walked over and laid a bottle of strawberry kiwi juice blend on the table. "And I got you a big, chewy chocolate chip cookie." She produced her prize with a flourish and laid it on the table beside the juice.

Jessie seemed unimpressed.

Meg looked at her, then at Drake. A frown crinkled her brow. "Is everything okay? She hasn't been bothering you, has she?"

"Not at all," he said, and got up to walk over to the wide windows looking over the city. "We were just getting to know each other, that's all."

That brought an even more worried look to Meg's face. "Know each other?" She looked back at Jessie. "What exactly did she say?" Her face had taken on a pink hue, a definite sign of her uneasiness.

On an impulse, Drake decided to seize on a once-in-a-lifetime opportunity. He and Meg would be seeing each other on a professional basis, but this might just be his chance to abandon professionalism for a while. He wanted the opportunity to be with her, speak to her, understand what he'd done that made her resent him so much.

"I can tell you all about it," he said, "if you'll agree to have dinner with me."

"Have din..." She stared at him, wide-eyed, then turned her suspicious gaze on her daughter. "Did you have something to do with this?"

Jessie turned her baby blues up to her mother and shook her head. "Unh-unh." "She didn't," Drake said, with a chuckle. "It was all my idea."

"See?" Jessie piped up. "I told you."

Meg looked back at Drake. "I don't know..." she began.

"Just say yes," Drake said, then he gave her a teasing grin. "Remember, I have information I'm sure you want."

Meg sucked in her breath then shook her head and exhaled. "You drive a hard bargain, Drake Duncan. All right, I'll do it, but just this one time."

One time is all I need. Drake gave a nod of triumph. "That's settled. then. Now let Jessie have her snack. We can squeeze in another half hour before I have to head out for my meeting."

Meg nodded and picked up her notepad.

As Drake turned to go back to his desk, his eyes caught Jessie's. She'd just taken a huge bite of her chocolate cookie and she gave him a wide, cookie-crumb smile.

He couldn't say for sure, but it certainly looked like little Jessie was on his side. Thank God for that. Where Meg Donovan-Gracey was concerned, he needed all the help he could get.

CHAPTER FIVE

The black one, the red one or the gold one? Heavens. The decisions a girl had to make.

It was Saturday night, a whole five days since Drake had asked her out, and she was in a pickle. It wasn't her dress she was worried about, although she still hadn't made up her mind which one to wear. It was the whole idea of going out with him that was driving her crazy. She'd agreed to go out with a man she'd hated – no, that was too strong a word – resented, for the past ten years, and all he'd done was ask her out and she'd given in.

Of course, there had been the issue of the information he'd promised to give her. What in the world had he and Jessie been talking about? She was dying of curiosity. Jessie tended to be a very vocal child and would say anything in front of practically anybody. Meg shuddered to think of what she'd said to Drake.

But it was now Saturday; she'd been pondering that question for the past five days. The other question was: was her need for the answer the only reason she'd accepted his invitation? She sincerely hoped that that was it. In her heart, though, she knew better. Her heart, that treacherous part of her, still had a very soft spot for this man she'd adored in her younger, immature days.

But goodness, she was older now, and far more experienced. She'd even been married to a man she'd loved and admired. So why did her heart pound at the thought of going out with a man who had hurt her so badly? She gave a deep sigh. Obviously, she had learned very little over the years, least of all how to protect her heart.

The babysitter came at six-thirty and at seven o'clock on the dot, she heard the doorbell ring.

"I'll get it," Jessie yelled and before Meg or Amelia could stop her, she was racing down the hallway toward the front door.

Meg grabbed her purse. "You have my cell phone number?"

"As always," Amelia said, with a roll of her eyes.

"Good. I'll only be a couple of hours, okay."

"No rush." Amelia pointed to her bag on the floor. "I have my laptop." "And call me in case of emer-"

"Mrs. Gracey. Please go." The young woman took her by the arm and turned her toward the door. "I've been babysitting Jessie for two years now. I know what I'm doing."

"Okay, okay. I'm going."
"Thank you." Amelia said, laughing at her.

Feeling just a little bit on the nervous side, Meg followed Jessie's path, and there, standing in the doorway, stood Drake, heart-stoppingly handsome in dark-gray suit, his shirt open at the collar. Goodness, he was almost Brad Pitt handsome, with his dark blond hair just touching the collar of his shirt.

"Hi, Drake," Jessie said, with a wave of her hand, then, "Bye, Drake," as she turned and ran back the way she had come.

"Mr. Duncan to you, missy," Meg called after her, but she'd already disappeared into the den where Amelia was waiting for her.

Now, Meg was completely alone with Drake, not dressed in business suit and sensible pumps like she'd been for their two previous meetings, but in elegant wear that reminded her that she was a woman. And he was a man. Going out on a date. Not exactly what she wanted to remember right now.

"Shall we go?" Drake gave her a polite nod then waited for her to step past him. His eyes had a special twinkle to them, and she could see that he liked what he saw. He didn't say anything, but somehow, he didn't need to. The eyes said it all.

Drake had chosen a restaurant which was only fifteen minutes' drive away from Meg's home, the Phancy Pheasant, one of her favorites. How had he known? It was an elegant place, and the food could only be described as exquisite. And it was pricey. Meg's visits to the restaurant had been rare but she'd enjoyed it immensely each time. After Greg's death she hadn't been back at all.

As they entered the lobby, the memories, so bittersweet, came rushing back, and Meg had to blink rapidly to clear the mist from her eyes.

"Are you all right?" Drake dipped his head to peer down at her.

"I'm...I'm fine," she said, in a choked whisper. Then, determined not to break down in from of him, she sniffed, straightened her back, and stepped ahead of him toward the hostess who was coming forward to greet them. To Meg's relief, she was able to regain control of her emotions and, just to make sure Drake didn't bug her with any more questions, she gave him her brightest smile. She was glad when he smiled back and seemed to relax. Danger averted. Thank goodness.

After the appetizer, they had a meal of the restaurant's signature dish, pheasant in wine on wild rice followed by chocolate mint and pistachio ice cream. Meg was dying to start questioning Drake about his conversation with Jessie but, not wanting to be rude, she bided her time, waiting for him to bring up the subject.

It was while they were sipping after-dinner tea, that he finally did. Drake gave her a slow smile then he rested his cup on the saucer and leaned back in his chair. "I think I've held you in suspense long enough," he said, with a wicked smile. "I'm ready to put you out of your misery if you'll promise me one thing."

Meg sat back in her chair and folded her arms across her chest. "Oh, no, you don't. Don't you dare tack on anything else. We had an arrangement. I go out to dinner with you, and you fill me in on everything you and Jessie talked about. That's it."

Drake chuckled. "You're right. Thought I could squeeze in something else along the way, but you caught me." Now it was Meg's turn to give him a wicked smile of her own. "Now, start talking. I'm all ears."

"Okay, Meg. I hope you can handle this." Drake sat forward, leaning toward her, and rested his arms on the table.

This sounded serious. Meg held her breath.

"Jessie told me about her father, and how he died. She also told me about her wish to have a daddy." Drake's eyes, so intensely gray, searched hers. It was as if he wanted to gauge her reaction. "She tells me she doesn't really remember her dad, but she seems to yearn for what she never had. She wants a complete family, Meg – mommy, daddy and baby."

Meg stared at Drake, at his brows now furrowed, his face serious. Strangely, he seemed genuinely concerned. "I know," she said, her voice almost a whisper, "But, her dad, we lost him..." her voice cracked, and she drew in a breath, "...we lost him when she was just a baby. All I can do is show her pictures and videos, and let her know how much he loved her."

Slowly, Drake nodded. "You're doing the right thing, to tell her all you can, about her dad. But she's asking for more, Meg. She wants a daddy, one who can be here with her."

"But...but..." She was stuttering now. For him to even mention that was useless. "What can I do about that? It's not like I can just pick one up off the store shelf, simply because my daughter wants one. A man is not a toy."

"True," Drake said, as he tented his fingers and stared across at her. "What if I told you I have the perfect solution to your problem?"

Her brows furrowed and she looked at him with suspicion.

"Which is?" "Marry me and give Jessie the daddy she wants."

Meg jerked forward, her body spasming in a fit of coughs. She'd half expected this suggestion, but she'd also thought he wouldn't be so audacious. The man must have gone totally insane. She took the glass he held out to her, and took several quick sips of water.

"What are you saying?" she finally squeaked.

"I'm saying, I want you to marry me."

Now, he was making her mad. "Drake, we only just met. What's it been? Three weeks?"

26 JUDY ANGELO

"I've known you for over ten years, Meg. I know you well enough to say, without any doubt, that I want you back in my life."

"Listen, Drake, you've taken this joke far enough." She picked up her napkin from her lap and dropped it on the table. "Either you drop this line of conversation, or you take me home right now."

"Meg, please." He held a hand up. "I'm sorry. I didn't mean to upset you. I just..." he shook his head and heaved a sigh, "...I just hoped I could make things right, get back to the place and time when you willingly gave me your all."

Now, why did he have to go and bring that up? He was digging up memories that were best forgotten. "I was young and stupid," she said, through clenched teeth. "I'm a mature woman now, and I know better."

"But a mature woman who still needs a man in her life."

Exasperated, Meg slapped her hands down on top of the linen-covered table. She glared at Drake. "Aren't you for- getting something?" Her voice rose to a slightly higher pitch as the anger climbed inside her. "You dumped me after taking my 'all', as you so elegantly put it." She drew in a shaky breath then looked around. Thank God, nobody seemed to have heard that. Now, she could truly appreciate the table that had been chosen for them – away from the others, secluded and out of earshot. Thank heavens for that.

"Drake Duncan, I've been waiting to say this for ten years." Meg leaned forward and spoke in a whisper that vibrated with her rage. "You used me, and then you left me, and I'll never forgive you."

There, she'd said it. All these years, she'd wanted to get that off her chest, and she'd finally gotten the chance. Now it was Drake Duncan's turn to explain himself. Not that it mattered anymore. There was nothing he could say that would erase her utter devastation at his callous rejection, nor the years of hurt that followed. It was only when she met Greg – God rest his soul – a mature man who was sixteen years her senior, but so understanding, so patient and so different from Drake, that she'd begun to heal.

Now, with those difficult years behind her, she could face Drake Duncan. She tilted her chin up and stared him straight in the eyes, expecting him to drop his gaze and duck his head in shame.

But he did not. Instead, on Drake's face was a look of confusion that she couldn't fathom. "What the devil are you talking about? You were the one who disappeared on me."

Meg gasped. The nerve of him, to lie right to her face. "I did not. I sat there in my dorm room your entire graduation night and you didn't even have the decency to come by and tell me you didn't want to be with me. You didn't come, and you didn't call. And even when I was leaving to catch my train the next morning, there was no sign of you." She gave an angry snort. "Now I know why they call some men dogs. You represented that pack very well."

Drake put his hand up and raked his fingers through his hair. When he looked at her again it was with a pained expression. "Meg, I have an explanation and an apology."

"Too late for that. You can't weasel-"

"No, hear me out." There was a firmness in his tone that made her stop and listen. "I did come back to see you, but I admit, I was late. I got caught up in all the graduation celebrations and family gatherings. I didn't get a chance to come back until next day. By that time, you had gone."

Her eyes narrowed as her heart went rigid. "Why should I believe you? You would probably say anything right now, just to get on my good side."

"If you don't believe me, ask your roommate. She was the one who told me you'd already left."

Meg frowned. The story was getting weirder by the second. "She did? But I called and spoke to her, and she never mentioned that you'd come."

"Well, I did. You can call and ask her now, if you want."

"No, I...I don't keep in touch with her anymore. I haven't spoken to her in years..." Her voice trailed off as the thought raced through her mind. Was he innocent of all she'd accused him of ? But then, there were other ways to get in touch with her, weren't there? If he'd really wanted to find her, he would have. With today's technology, there was no excuse. "So, why didn't you track me down?" she demanded. "You could have, but you didn't want to."

DADDY BY DECEMBER 27

He dropped his eyes then. Finally, he was showing shame.
"No," he said, his voice low, "I didn't want to."

His words were like a punch to her stomach. "You...didn't want to,"
she said, in a choked whisper, "and now you have the audacity to sit
there and ask me to marry you?"

He looked back at her then. He shook his head, seeming almost
impatient that she'd asked the question. "You said I was a jerk who you
wouldn't touch with a long stick. You told her that I'd shown my true
colours, and that you hated me. and you never wanted to see me again."

The truth will always come out. Meg bit her lower lip then released
it. "Yes," she said quietly, "I did say that. But what about the rest? Did
she tell you what else I said?"

"That was it, but that was all I needed to hear. Do you think
I'm a sucker for punishment?"

"No, but if you'd stayed to hear the rest, then you'd have known
that I told her I loved you with all my heart and that was why it hurt
so much when you rejected me. I felt so cheap." Her voice caught in a
hiccup. "You don't understand."

"I...do." He sighed, and his face grew somber. "And I also
understand how immature and stupid I was, even though I was a
graduating senior. I just took everything your roommate said, at face
value." He gave a hiss fraught with frustration. "I should have known,
but when she told me what you' would said, I was hurt and angry. I
guess not trying to find you was my way of hurting you back. In the
end, we both suffered."

For a long while, they stared at each other in silence, each reliving
that night that had so changed their lives. How differently it could have

turned out if they hadn't both been too angry and too hurt to reach out and find each other?

Then, it all became too much for her. "I...have to go. Can you take me home, please?" She shook her head and dropped her eyes, refusing to look at him. She wasn't ready for this revelation. Her mind in turmoil, she wanted to get home, where she could go off somewhere by herself and think.

"Will you think about my question?" Drake's voice was gentle.

Meg didn't answer. She reached for her purse. "Please. Let's just go."

Thank goodness he did not object. Drake called for the bill, and within minutes, they were walking back to his car. And when he walked her to her door, there was no attempt at intimacy – no touch, no kiss. Thank God for that. Because tonight had turned her entire world upside down, and she had no idea where she should go from here.

WELL, THAT HAD GONE well.

His thoughts turning sarcastic, Drake's lips twisted in a smile of irony as he thought about his last encounter with Meg. It had been four days since they'd gone out to dinner, and he hadn't heard a word from her. He'd tried calling her at home, only once, but he'd only heard a recorded message. He hadn't bothered to leave a message. He would be seeing her on Thursday, anyway. That appointment was already set. There was no way he was going to let her escape him again.

But although he had every intention of going for what he wanted – and what he wanted was Meg – there was still that nagging doubt at the back of his mind. He wanted her...but did she want him? In her heart, had she moved on, so far away that he could never win her again? Dammit, the thought was driving him crazy. To know that it might be too late...no, it did not bear thinking about.

With a grunt, he got up from the desk and went over to the closet, where he grabbed his gym bag then dug his cell phone out of his pocket and dialed. "Tyson, it's late, and I know you're still in the office, stuck in front of that damn computer. Meet me in my gym. Twenty minutes. Take your gear."

The earpiece came alive with protest. Tyson, his friend from college, was the consummate workaholic. Drake often had to literally drag him away from the computer, and then, when he got a chance, he would pull out his iPad or smart phone. The man always had to be connected to something. This evening, though, Drake wanted to see his friend, not just to make sure he was not overworking, but to talk, and when he needed to talk, Tyson was the only friend he could trust when it came to matters of the heart.

Drake rode the elevator down to his private gym in the basement of the building, where he changed quickly and did a few rounds of push-ups. He was doing crunches when the door opened and Tyson, tall and dark and lean, walked into the room.

Drake grinned. "How goes it, old man?" he asked, his voice breathless as he continued to crunch his abs as he lay on the floor. "Making some greenbacks on the market?"

Tyson grinned back, as he shucked his sweatshirt and flexed his muscles. "Can't complain, old man, can't complain." He walked over to the stationary bike. "Glad you called me when you did. With all the work I have piled up, I'd probably be at the office till past midnight."

"Yup, I know you. And if you're not careful, that beautiful wife of yours is going to leave you." He exhaled with a puff of air, then sat up. "Remember this, man, money isn't everything."

Tyson burst out laughing. "Well spoken by a man worth over a billion and who has no woman to share it with." That stung, but Drake did not let it show. He gave a chuckle, then said, "In time, man. In time."

After that, Tyson and Drake got serious, spending the next thirty minutes lifting weights and spotting each other, working up a sweat that left the shirts of both men soaked through with sweat.

It was not until they were cooling down, doing light after-workout exercises, that Drake dropped the bomb on Tyson. "I found her, man. After years of waiting, I've found 'the one'."

"What the-" Tyson stopped and stared at him. "When did this happen?" "Three weeks ago."

His friend frowned, obviously confused. "Say what?"

"Well, to be more accurate, ten years ago. She's someone I met in college. I never thought I would see her again, but then she just walked right back into my life." He glanced at Tyson. "Call me a psycho, but I think it's fate."

"Yeah," Tyson snorted, "or she found out you're worth a fortune, and wants a cut."

Drake frowned. He almost felt like punching him for that one. He would let it pass, though, because Tyson didn't know Meg. No-one could look her in the eye and doubt her sincerity. "She didn't come looking for me," he said. "I was the one who did the hunting. Well, sort of."

Now, Tyson looked even more perplexed. "Explain yourself," he demanded.

And that was when, without giving her name, Drake described the happy coincidence where the woman he'd fallen for ten years earlier had been the one chosen to write his memoir. When he was done sharing the story, he walked over to the bench against the wall and plopped down, a sudden feeling of despondence washing over him. He began to loosen the laces on his gym shoes.

"For someone who's just reunited with the love of his life, you don't look too happy." Tyson leaned against the treadmill and folded his arms across his chest. "What gives?"

Drake was staring at his feet, his thoughts going back to his last conversation with Meg, then he exhaled heavily. "I asked her to marry me."

Tyson gave a start, and when Drake looked up, his work-out partner was staring at him as if he'd grown two heads. Maybe three. "Are you out of your flippin' mind? Didn't you meet her, like three weeks ago?"

"Three weeks and ten years," Drake said drily.

"Yeah, yeah. But people change, man. Do you know what she's been up to, these past ten years?"

"Don't need to." Drake stared into Tyson's eyes. "What I need, is to bounce something off you. She didn't give me a yes or a no. In fact, the way she practically cut me to shreds with her eyes, I think it's a safe bet that the answer is no." He frowned as he recalled her reaction. "You're the expert on women. What do I do? Back off and give her some space, or put on the pressure till she gives in? I blew it once before. I can't afford to do that again."

DADDY BY DECEMBER 29

Tyson stared down at him. "You're serious?"

"Very."

Tyson nodded, then walked over and sat on the other end of the bench. "Then, here's what you do..."

CHAPTER SIX

M eg drew in a deep breath, then let it out slowly. She picked up the leather briefcase from the seat beside her, pulled her coat tighter around her, then got out of the car. "Well, here goes," she whispered under her breath.

This would be her first appointment with Drake since their dinner and that awkward conversation, and she wasn't looking forward to the meeting. She still couldn't believe the man had asked her to marry him. What if he brought up the subject again? Heavens, she hoped he didn't. If that first time had been uncomfortable, then a second time, she would just die from embarrassment because...she didn't have an answer for him.

She honestly didn't know why she was even worrying herself about it. The logical answer was no. First, he had hurt her terribly – however unintentional – and second, there had been a ten year gap between their brief encounter and now. Who ever heard of picking up where you left off...ten years later?

Meg sighed, her head full of questions for which there were no answers. But, although her mind was in total turmoil, she kept her face bland. She had a job to do, and she was going into Drake's office, the perfect professional. When he saw she was all about business and nothing else, he wouldn't dare bring up that contrary topic again.

But later, as she sat across from Drake to interview him on a particularly risky business venture, Meg couldn't help but wonder if she hadn't done too good a job in projecting a no-nonsense image. If she thought she would be cool and businesslike, Drake was even more so. He almost seemed aloof, his face not showing a flicker of emotion, her tone clipped and curt. It was as if Saturday night had never happened.

Where was the man who had begged her to marry him? Well, maybe 'begged' was too strong a word; but he'd asked.

Meg frowned. She hadn't dreamed the whole thing. Or had she? She shook her head, distracted and frustrated all at once, and trained her eyes and her attention back on Drake. The heat rose in her face as she saw his sardonic smile. He knew she was perturbed by his behaviour. He knew she'd expected

him to continue where he'd left off. But he'd done the exact opposite.

When the hour finally came to a close, Meg slipped her notes back into her case and zipped it shut. "Thank you," she said, her voice as formal as she could make it. "I'll be back next Thursday to wrap up this section."

"Sounds good," Drake said, with a nod. "I'll see you then." Then he got up and walked her to the door, and that was that.

Wow. Meg sat in her car and stared straight ahead, trying to figure out what had just happened. It was like she was in the presence of another man. She let out her breath slowly and started the car.

Well, so much for wanting to marry her. It was obvious that, right now, that idea was the farthest thing from his mind. She could just kiss that dream bye-bye.

The following week, when Meg showed up at Drake's office, she was better prepared for his cool reception. She'd steeled herself to accept it, but no matter how strong she thought she was, it was still hard to think that he could have gotten over her so easily. As she sat in the chair in front of Drake, she swallowed, then took out her notepad and slid her recorder out of her bag. She frowned as she struggled to focus.

Buck up, woman, this is work and nothing else. It's what's feeding you and Jessie right now so be happy.

After that personal pep talk, Meg forced a smile to her lips and got the interview going.

To her surprise, at the end of the session as she rose to leave, Drake stopped her with an unexpected question. "How is the little princess?"

"Jessie?"

"Of course, who else?" he said, with a smile.

"Oh, she's...fine. She's at Kids' Club right now. It's a special art program where they learn to paint and sketch." Drake raised an eyebrow. "Sounds like fun."

DADDY BY DECEMBER 31

Meg relaxed her rigid pose for the first time since she got there. "Well, Jessie certainly thinks so. She loves all the activities."

"That's great," he said, with what looked like sincerity. "Tell her I said hi."

"I will."

This time when he walked her to the door, the air didn't crackle quite so much with tension. It was definitely an improvement to their previous meeting. Not exactly the kind of attention she'd been expecting since his interest seemed to be only with Jessie, but she could live with that.

The following week, to Meg's chagrin, she had to cancel. She'd totally forgotten about the parent teacher conference at Jessie's school. She was a volunteer, and one on which the PTA had come to rely heavily, so, as far as the association was concerned, her absence from the meeting was not an option.

She'd considered disappointing them anyway, but when she called Drake and explained the clash, he very graciously offered to postpone his session with her. If she should admit it to herself, she had to say that she was a little disappointed that he hadn't even tried to convince her to still come in. It was great that he was flexible, but was she the only one doing the missing?

Holy Moses. She'd just admitted to herself that she missed – as in M-I-S-S-E-D – Drake Duncan. Okay, now she knew she was really in trouble. What kind of a crazy woman would be missing a man who only saw her as a note-taker, scribe, writer of memoirs, whatever, but not how she wanted to be seen – as an attractive woman he couldn't stop thinking about?

Stop it, Meg. Stop it this instant. Missing Drake is absolutely out of the question.

But it was easier said than done. Over the several weeks that she'd been seeing him, although on a professional level, he'd grown on her, her perverse heart pounding each time she thought of seeing him again.

By the time the following Thursday came around, she was so jittery that she dropped her pen twice before she got to Drake's floor of the building. She stopped outside his office door and drew in a deep breath. How old was she again? Was it thirty, twenty or was she a silly teen? Sadly, she was acting like the last of the three...and all because she hadn't seen him in the space of two weeks.

She picked up her courage from where it had fallen on the floor and tucked it into her pocket. There. Ready to roll.

She tapped on the door.

At the sound of his voice, Meg pushed the door open, and entered the now familiar office with its wide glass windows and impressive view of the city below, the shimmering blue lake as its backdrop. Her eyes quickly scanned the expansive room and then settled on Drake, who had been sitting at his desk, but was now rising to greet her.

She was pleasantly surprised to see that today he was more casual than usual, wearing a navy sports jacket with pale blue shirt open at the collar. His hair, too, was different. He seemed to be growing it longer because today it curled at his neck in a disturbingly sexy sort of way. She almost groaned. Sheer torture.

It was torture that she couldn't just drop her briefcase on the floor, walk up to him, and reach out to slide her fingers through that glossy blond hair; torture that she couldn't grip the back of his head and force it down till those lips met hers in a kiss so hot and hungry that it would make her forget her own name; torture that she couldn't shove him back into his chair and...

Jesus, Meg, get a hold of yourself. You've been celibate for too long.

"...feels like it's been a month," he was saying.

Meg blinked. "Pardon me?"

Drake smiled, a delectable smile that had her heart speeding up. "I was saying that it feels like I haven't seen you for a month, not just two weeks."

A month, he said? Try a year. The way her body was reacting to him, it was like she'd been craving his touch for a long, long time.

32 JUDY ANGELO

And when he did connect with her, just to shake her hand, she knew what the romance novels meant when they said the girl melted at his touch. Heck, she'd even written that into her own stories. Now, she knew exactly what it felt like.

When he let go, she sank gratefully into the chair he'd pulled out for her then, surreptitiously, she drew in some breaths to clear her head.

"We're almost there," he said with a smile so warm that it caught her off guard. So, where was the iceberg that had greeted her those last two meetings? In its place was a man so relaxed and cordial and gorgeous, that she was having a hard time keeping her eyes off him. "After this interview, I guess your focus will be on converting all those notes into a story."

"Correct," she said, glad he'd started a conversation. She needed the distraction. "After today, I'll be spending the next several weeks working on the first draft."

"A lot of work and creativity," he said, as he gave her a look of admiration. "Don't worry. I won't be calling every few days to ask how far along you are. I'll just leave you to do what you do best."

Call me, Drake. Bug me. Get on my nerves. I can deal with anything except your silence.

"Thank you," she said quietly. "I appreciate your understanding."

That day, the last of the interview days – at least, for a while – the session went for over an hour and a half and when she was done, Meg closed her notebook and gave Drake a triumphant smile. It was mostly triumphant at having completed phase I of the project, but a little wobbly when she recalled that she wouldn't see Drake that often anymore...if at all...unless they had to tie up some loose ends.

She started packing her papers and books back into the briefcase, wondering how she would say goodbye, when Drake's voice stopped her.

"So, what are you and Jessie doing this weekend?"

She paused, her papers halfway into the bag on her lap, and looked up at him. The question caught her off guard and she had to stop and think for a moment. "We were planning to go to the aquarium on Sunday and maybe the museum. It's still too cold to do much outside."

He nodded. "True. But I see that despite the temperature, you've found ways to keep Jessie occupied. I like that."

She smiled. "Thanks."

"And," he continued, "if you don't think I'm being too presumptuous, I would love to tag along."

"Really?' She stared at him, incredulous. As much as the idea appealed to her, she just couldn't picture this suave tycoon trudging behind a five-year-old and her not-so-young-anymore mother. She chuckled inwardly at that thought.

"Really," he said, with a laugh. "And you don't need to look so shocked. I'm human, you know."

"I know," she said, smiling back. "After all the information I gathered on you, I know you like you're my brother." "Or lover," he said, and gave her a look so full of promise that her heart jerked in her chest.

"What time should I pick you up?" he asked.

No backing out now. "Ten-thirty should be fine," she said, accepting defeat.

But it was a defeat that sent a thrill running through her entire body. Drake Duncan was going to spend Sunday with her. Oh, and

Jessie, of course. Mainly Jessie. But no matter if his focus was not on her, just being with him was going to make Sunday a heck of a great day.

DADDY BY DECEMBER 33

"WHY DO YOU DO THIS to me, man? I told you, I don't like dressing up to go to rub shoulders with the rich and famous." Tyson James glared at Drake as he loosened his cuffs and began to roll back his sleeves.

Unconcerned that his friend looked ready to throw a hissy fit, Drake chuckled. "Talking about the rich and famous, you're not so shabby yourself."

"That's beside the point. You know I hate it when you invite me to your parent's house. You guys are old money. I'm new money. Old and new don't mix very well."

At that, Drake laughed out loud. "That's a ten-ton load of bull and you know it. Mom and Dad love you. Too much, if you ask me. I'm beginning to get a bit jealous." He fell silent as the server approached their table with two mugs of beer then, drinks served, he turned his attention back to Tyson. "It's my birthday, so suck it up. Tomorrow. Four-thirty."

It was Friday night, and as they did every now and then, Drake and Tyson swung by Simpson's, an exclusive sports bar not far from Navy Pier. It was the perfect place to unwind after a long and hectic week.

"Tyson grinned. "You're getting old, man, real old."

"Thirty-four? Perfect age. Young enough to be called young, old enough to not make too many stupid mistakes." Drake shrugged. "And it's not like you're any younger. Thirty-five in August, right?"

Tyson laughed. "You got me." Then, as his chuckle died away, he turned curious eyes on Drake. "So, how are things with the love of your life?"

Drake leaned forward and picked up the frothing mug. He took a sip of his beer. "Going good, I'm guessing." "You're guessing?"

"It's early days yet, so I don't want to make any premature calls, but she looks like she's coming around." Drake shrugged. "At least, she hasn't slammed the door in my face. I'll be spending Sunday with her."

"Sweet." Tyson gave him a look of triumph. "I told you – back off, give the lady some breathing room, and slowly work your way back in. It worked, didn't it?"

"So far, so good."

"You damned near scared her away for good, dropping the marriage bombshell on the table like that." Tyson shook his head. "Glad you took my advice and stepped back and gave her a chance to miss you, let her see you in a different light. So...Sunday, huh?"

"No need to look so smug." Drake shook his head at Tyson. "It will be three of us. Her little girl will be there. We're going to the aquarium."

"Oh." Tyson looked a little deflated but then his face cleared. "That's okay. It's a start. And I have the perfect plan-"

"Whoa, hold up, buddy. No more plans. I took your advice when I was desperate, but from here on, it's my call."

CHAPTER SEVEN

"**D**rake!"

Drake heard a yell and was just in time to catch the tiny body dressed in pink that had hurled itself at him. Jessie flew into his arms and, laughing at her excitement, he lifted her high into the air, making her squeal with delight.

As he gently placed her to stand on the ground, he looked up and saw Meg, rosy-cheeked and smiling, as she walked down the driveway toward them. She'd pulled her hair up in a ponytail, which made her look all of sixteen. Gone was the sophisticated lady he'd come to know, in her smart business suits and immaculate make-up. Today, her face looked fresh and bare, her skin glowing in the bright spring sunshine.

"Good morning." She greeted him with an infectious smile.
"Morning yourself," he said, as he smiled down at her. "Ready to roll?"

"Yup." She nodded. "Just as soon as I get Jessie's booster seat from my car."

In less than two minutes, they had Jessie buckled up in Drake's SUV and he was backing out of their driveway. Then, they were on their way. He and Meg didn't do much in the way of conversation, but they didn't have to. Jessie kept up a running commentary, telling them about her week at Kids' Camp, all the drawing she'd done and the friends she'd made. She didn't stop talking until they pulled into the parking lot of the aquarium.

"Yay," the little girl yelled, almost bouncing out of her booster seat in her excitement. "We're here, Mommy, we're here."

"I know, honey." Meg looked back and smiled at her daughter. "Now, just stay calm and we'll have you out of the car in a jiffy."

They got out of the car and as they walked toward the building with Jessie holding Meg's hand, he almost laughed out loud as he watched them.

Jessie, in her eagerness, was dragging her mother forward, making her almost have to break into a trot to keep up. Meg raised her voice in protest but Jessie refused to slow down. Finally, Drake had to come to her rescue.

"Okay, Jessie, let's be good now. You need to listen to your mother."

Jessie stopped immediately and turned to look back at him with big, blue eyes that were full of reproach. Maybe it was because this was only her third time meeting him, or maybe it was the sound of a male voice. Drake couldn't tell which, but after that, Jessie calmed right down and began walking sedately by her mother's side.

He smiled to himself as he followed behind. It felt good to be out on a sunny day for a family excursion. And that was what it felt like – family. Was this what he'd been missing all this time? Tyson had often teased him about being a loner and he'd never let it bother him too much. It wasn't as if he was short of women to go out with. But this, he'd never had before. And he wanted more.

"Hey guys, wait up," he called out. He caught up with them and together they began their sightseeing journey, exploring the mysteries of the ocean deep.

From stingrays to sharks to belugas, they saw them all. They had to pull Jessie away from the dolphins she loved so much. Then, they explored the Caribbean reefs, with their strange and sometimes scary-looking inhabitants – sea turtles, spiny lobsters and the ominous-looking moray eels.

After Jessie had had her fill of jellyfish and octopuses, they took a lunch break then set off for the children's museum. There, Jessie had a ball, conducting science experiments, building architectural structures, and her favorite, drawing. When the presenter announced that they would be showing a movie about how the earth was formed Jessie was the first among the children to jump up and raise her hand. Drake smiled as he watched her, so bold and confident. There was not an ounce of shyness in her.

34

DADDY BY DECEMBER 35

"PARENTS," THE UNIFORMED attendant called out, "please make yourselves comfortable in the waiting lounge. The movie will only take forty-five minutes. We have one caretaker of every sixth child, so your little one will be fine."

Meg's eyes widened in surprise, and she turned to look at Drake. "That long? I hope she can sit through it."

"I'm sure she will," Drake said, with confidence. From what he'd seen of Jessie, he had no doubt that she would adapt to her situation. "Don't worry. She'll be fine. Let's grab a seat by the windows."

Meg seemed to take his word for it because she relaxed visibly then walked ahead of him, heading for the seats along the plate glass windows. She plopped down onto the padded bench and patted the seat beside her. "We might as well relax," she said, with a crooked smile. "We have a long wait."

For a moment, Drake just stared at her as the brilliant smile lit up her face. Maybe it was just him. He was probably in a state of euphoria, but as she smiled, all he could think was, *I want this woman in my life. What will it take to get her to marry me?*

Whatever it took, he would do it. He'd been waiting ten years and three months now, and this time he would not let go until the woman smiling at him became Mrs. Meg Duncan.

WHY IS HE STARING AT me like that? Meg's smile wavered as she tried to figure out the strange expression on Drake's face. His body was here, but with that faraway look in his eyes and that half smile, she could see that his mind was miles away. Then, as if suddenly snapping out of a trance, he shook his head and began walking over to the bench where she was already sitting.

"Are you all right?" she asked, as he sat down beside her.

"Perfect," he replied, and she could not dispute it, when she saw the pleased expression on his face. Whatever he'd been thinking about, had certainly made him a happy man.

And for what it was worth, she was happy, too. She was having a wonderful time with two people whose company she enjoyed most – her beloved Jessie, and now this man who was beginning to steal her heart, a little piece at a time. And there was nothing she could do to stop him.

Dressed in khaki slacks and a soft brown wool sweater, he looked both casual and cultured at the same time. She loved the way his gray eyes sparkled as he laughed with Jessie. He seemed to have so much fun with her. Who would have known that the big-shot billionaire would actually take the time to make her daughter feel special? She'd listened to hours of narration about his life, had taken the notes and prepared the outline, but nothing he'd said had given her as authentic a picture of who he was as the hours he'd spent with her child. She was seeing a side to him which she was sure few knew existed.

As Drake slid back onto the seat all the way and crossed his arms, Meg looked down at her hands. Okay, so he was here beside her. Now what? Were they going to spend the next forty-five minutes just staring out the window? Her mind raced, trying to find a topic of conversation that would interest him. What did men like to talk about, outside of sports, cars and women? She knew very little about the first two, and for the third, she could hardly have a conversation with a man about women.

She cleared her throat then glanced over at him. "So...since we left college,, you've been pretty busy building your investment empire."

He shrugged. "You know all the details. I'm counting on you to pump some excitement into the boring story of my life."

She narrowed her gaze as she looked at him. "You became a billionaire in under ten years, and you call that boring?

I should be so lucky."

"Hey, you can be a billionaire writer. Look at J. K. Rowling. I'll be looking for your name on that list next."

36 JUDY ANGELO

"Yeah, right," she said, with a laugh.

After that, they fell silent again, with him staring at the people milling around in the lobby at the end of the hall, and her alternating between staring at her hands and out the window.

Finally, she decided to be brave, daring to ask him about that part of himself he had not shared with her during the interviews. "Uhm...may I ask you a personal question, Drake?"

"Sure," he said, as he turned toward her. "Go ahead."

"For a man as successful as you...and as handsome...why didn't you ever get married?" She could feel herself turn red even as the words left her mouth. She'd actually asked the question that had been on her mind all this time. Holy cow. What must he think of her? Miss Nosy Parker, he was probably saying in his mind.

She didn't regret asking the question, though. Ten years was a long time for a man as attractive as he was to stay unattached. She was curious. But when she got his response, it stopped her cold.

"I was."

She gasped. "You was...I mean, you were? You were married?"

He nodded, and gave her a smile that seemed full of regret. "Yes, a long time ago."

"Did she...pass away?" He looked so sad that she had no doubt he'd lost someone he'd loved dearly. As unfair as it was, the thought made her heart hurt. He'd loved someone besides her? The green-eyed monster was rearing its ugly head.

"No, nothing like that." He shook his head. "She lives on, and very comfortably, I might add." "You're divorced, then."

He sighed. "A more accurate word is annulled." "What happened?"

He looked away then he tightened his lips. "The marriage lasted all of three days." He sighed. "I was stupid. I started dating a woman I met at a business conference. Only two months into the relationship, she announced she was pregnant."

He'd spluttered when Claudia had given him the news and she'd laughed at his shock. "Those things happen some- times, Drake," she'd told him. Of course, he knew that, but they'd used protection. But, then again, condoms weren't one hundred percent protection. She'd insisted they get married within the next month. She wanted to be married before her pregnancy became obvious. He hadn't objected.

As Meg watched Drake as he told his story, she could see his face grow rigid, and there was a bitter twist to his mouth.

She could tell that what was to come would not be good.

"We left the next day for our honeymoon," he said. "The south of France; her choice. I didn't really care."

"We booked the presidential suite in the grandest hotel, La Belle Provence. The day after we arrived, I got out of bed fairly early, and told her I was going for a jog to work off some of my jetlag and wake myself up. She just groaned and rolled over and went back to sleep." Drake drew in a deep breath then exhaled slowly. "At least, that was what I thought."

Meg frowned. That sounded ominous. She was dying to know what happened next, but when he fell silent, she did not push. He needed to tell his story in his own time.

"It wasn't till I got down to the lobby that I realized I'd left my cell phone." Drake was not looking at Meg now. He stared straight ahead as he spoke, looking as if he'd been transported back in time. "I was quiet, going back into the suite. I didn't want to wake her. I'd just grabbed the phone from the coffee table, when I thought I heard voices coming from the bedroom. I decided to check."

His jaw tightened and he spoke through clenched teeth as he said the next words. "She was on the phone, talking about how she'd 'bagged' me with a fake pregnancy. Said she was going to wait another week or two before telling me about the miscarriage. Of course, she was going to make that up, too."

"Oh, my God." Meg's hand flew to her mouth. How could a woman be so devious?

DADDY BY DECEMBER 37

"Apparently, it had all been a set-up. The whirlwind romance, the rushed marriage. She'd targeted me long before I even knew she existed. Based on the rest of the conversation, it seemed the plan had been in place for over a year."

Drake shook his head. "I got rid of her so fast she didn't know what hit her." Then, he laughed, and the sound was harsh and bitter. "That's the last time I'll let a woman make a fool out of me." He snorted. "Pregnancy. I fell for the age-old trick." He shook his head again then, to Meg's relief, he chuckled. "Let's hope that now that I'm the ripe old age of thirty-four, I won't fall for a stupid trick like that again."

She laughed with him, but inside she was pained by what he'd gone through. The nerve of that woman, to try to trap him with a baby. In this case, a fake one. Some women would stop at nothing to trap a rich man into marriage.

Trying to lighten the mood, she decided to change the subject. "I started writing chapter one this week. It's going great."

As she'd expected, his face brightened. "Good. I'm looking forward to seeing your first draft."

"We're still a couple of months away from a full draft, but I'm happy with the way it started off. It's really flowing." "Great."

"I'm depicting you like the urban version of the swashbuckling cowboy of the wild west." "What?"

"You're the one who said I should add excitement to your boring life. Well, I'm doing that." She was smiling now. "I don't know..." he said, putting his hand to his chin. "Do you really think-"

"Got you." She burst out laughing. "You're so gullible."

By this time, he was laughing, too. "My one major flaw. I need to work on that."

After that, the tension dissipated, and it was as if Drake had never brought up the sensitive subject of his disaster marriage at the hands of a femme fatale. They fell into comfortable conversation and lost track of time, so that when Jessie burst into the waiting lounge with the rest of her group in tow, they looked at each other, surprised.

"Has it been forty-five minutes already?" Meg couldn't help asking. "Guess so," Drake said, then opened his arms as Jessie ran toward him.

She hopped onto his lap as if she'd been doing that all her life, then whipped a toy out of her pocket. "Look what I got. A baby dinosaur." She reached over and shook the green soft toy under Meg's nose. "Here, Mommy, I'll let you play with it first."

"Thank you, sweetie." Meg took it and smiled her gratitude.

"Hey, didn't you bring me anything?" Drake put on a sad face and even added a pout.

Meg had to laugh. He was actually a good actor. *Move over, Brad Pitt.*

"I'm sorry, I only got one toy," Jessie said, her eyes full of regret. "Don't be sad. You can play with it after Mommy's done. I'll go last, okay."

"You're such a sweetheart," Drake said. "Now you've made me so happy, I don't even need a dinosaur anymore. Not when I have you to play with." And he tickled her till she giggled and writhed and squealed for him to stop.

That evening as Drake drove them home with Jessie snoring softly in the back, Meg leaned back in her seat and sighed. It had been a wonderful day and she could not have asked for more. Did she dare hope that he would spend more time with them? She would love many more days like this, and so would Jessie, she was sure.

For now, though, she would savor the afterglow of this one. She glanced over at Drake as he drove and, as if he felt her eyes on him, he looked across at her and smiled.

And that smile, simple as it seemed, was all it took to make her spirit soar.

CHAPTER EIGHT

M teg was on a high for days after the outing with Drake. She was in such a good mood that she'd got up before dawn each morning and worked for three solid hours before Jessie even began to stir. Then, once she'd dropped her off at school, she'd gone right back on the job, not budging from her computer until it was time to get Jessie. Then, when her daughter was asleep, she worked for two or three hours more, as if she'd been shot with a double dose of adrenalin. For two weeks, she kept up the pace so that, long before the date she'd set, she had Drake's first draft ready.

During this productive period, Drake called a few times, and each time she'd been happy to give him a positive progress report. What made her even happier was that he never forgot to ask for Jessie.

Finally, the day came when she would see him again. She would be presenting him with the completed first draft of his memoir. First, though, she had to drop her daughter off at her parents' house in Woodridge. The little girl would be spending the weekend with her grandparents, as she did every so often. She loved roaming the wide-open spaces of her grandparents' property and playing with the many pets they had. She loved Alexis, the German Shepherd, and Caleb, the rooster, but her absolute favorite was Sasha, the Siamese cat who was queen of the home. She was a mild-mannered cat who would allow Jessie to put a bonnet on her head and place her in her toy pram and push her around the yard.

"Yay," Jessie yelled, as they pulled into the yard.

Before Meg even got a chance to go around and open the door for her, Jessie had pulled her seatbelt, opened the door and hopped out. She dashed up the winding gravel road.

"Wait for me," Meg called to her, but as usual, Jessie had more pressing things on her mind than waiting for her mom. Meg sighed and opened the back door to get Jessie's bag then she followed her daughter at a slower pace. As she climbed the steps, Jessie rang the bell.

The door opened immediately. Patrick and Juliet Donovan stood in the doorway, all smiles. Patrick bent down to gather his only grandchild into his arms, while Meg stepped into her mother's hug. Then, she dropped Jessie's bag in the corner.

"I've got to go, guys. I have a meeting downtown." She leaned over to her daughter who still clung to her grandfather's shoulder.

"Kiss?"

Meg was awarded with a big, fat, wet one on the cheek.

An hour later, Meg arrived at Drake's office, the completed first draft in hand. For the first time since she'd been visiting his office, he was late. She was sitting alone in the waiting lounge, absorbed in a story on her Kindle e-book reader, when a deep voice made her jump.

"I would love to know what you're reading."

When Meg looked up, Drake was smiling down at her, his briefcase still in hand. He looked like he'd just come in from a meeting.

"You should have seen your face," he said. "I hope I didn't catch you in the middle of a love scene."

Meg could feel her face color, but she got up and laughed it off. "Only a mild one," she said, as she picked up her bag. Actually, he'd guessed right. She'd been enjoying the love scene of a juicy romance novel and it had been anything but mild.

"Sorry I'm late," he said, as they headed for his office. "My meeting went longer than expected."

"Not a problem. Business first," she said, giving him a cheeky look, "or else you won't be able to pay me the balance on my ghostwriting fee. So, meet away."

He laughed at that. "There may be a recession on, but I think I'll be able to manage your fee."

They settled down in the office and skimmed through the first few chapters together, with Drake filling in the blanks for some areas where she'd had questions. But then, in the middle of the fourth chapter he stopped her.

"I've been talking all day. I could do with a drink. What would you like?"
"Oh, ginger ale please, if you have it."

Drake's office was equipped with an alcove into which he disappeared. When he came out, he was carrying two cans of ginger ale and two glasses filled with ice. After he'd served her, he walked over to the plush sofa by the window and sank into it with a sigh.

"Long day?" she asked, as she took a sip of the bubbly liquid.

"Yes, one of those days." He began to loosen his tie, then he stopped and looked at her. "Do you mind?" "Not at all."

He pulled off the tie and opened a couple of buttons at his collar, revealing just a hint of broad chest, then he sighed and relaxed into the chair. He took a long drink of his ginger ale. "I needed that." He rested the glass on the coffee table. "How's Jessie? Created any art masterpieces lately?"

"She's fine, thanks. She's working on a paper mache duck at school this week, so she took it with her to show my parents."

"Oh, she's with her grandparents today?"

"For the weekend," Meg told him. "I like to let her spend time with them every few weeks. The house is big, and there's a lot of space where she can play. She and the neighbourhood kids are good friends, too. She loves going there to play."

Drake nodded as he sat forward and rested his elbows on his knees. "I guess she gets lonely sometimes, not having a sibling to play with?"

"You've got that right," Meg said emphatically. "She keeps pestering me for a little brother or sister. I don't know why, because she's now old enough to know it takes a mommy and a daddy to make a baby..." Her voice trailed off, and her heart did a skip as she stared at Drake. Now, how had she ended up down that garden path? What had they been talking about again?

Meg breathed a sigh of relief when Drake rescued her from the foot she'd put in her mouth. "Have you ever heard of the South African Dance Troupe, The Leaping Lions?"

She shook her head. "No, never."

"I've seen them perform once. Excellent group. They'll be in Wisconsin this Saturday, performing in Muskego, a small town just outside of Milwaukee. Would you like to go with me?"

"To Milwaukee? That's two hours away."

"So?" he said with a shrug. "It's the weekend. We can take our time and cruise over to Wisconsin, then cruise right back. It will be a nice drive."

She thought about it a moment. Of course, she would love to go. She hadn't gone out in ages, and to see an international dance group? That had to be good. But the question was, what effect would it have on her? With each passing week, it was as if she'd grown more and more emotionally attached to this man. But, one day, the memoir project would be over, and then what? She knew she'd better be careful, or else she would be in for a bad fall. And going out on a second date with Drake might just be the thing to send her over that cliff.

"I don't know..." she began, but she stopped when he held up his hand.

"Give me one good reason why you can't come," he said, a look of challenge in his eyes. "You don't have Jessie to worry about. You're almost done with my project, and you have the whole weekend ahead of you."

Well, aren't wee sure of ourself? She cocked an eyebrow at him. "And what if I already have a date?"

That one seemed to knock him off balance. He blinked, then a slight frown creased his brow. "Oh, sorry. I hadn't thought of that."

He looked so worried, that Meg had to put him out of his misery. "All right, I admit it. I don't have a date. And I don't have much of an excuse not to go."

"So, you'll go with me?" He had an eager look that made him look a whole lot younger.

40 JUDY ANGELO

"Yes," she said, with a note of finality, "I'll go with you." Best to say yes before she changed her mind. If she didn't go, she would spend the rest of her days regretting it. And you only live once, right? That settled, she smiled at him. "What time should I be ready?"

"I'll pick you up at four-thirty," he said. "I like to give myself an extra hour, just in case of heavy traffic."

"I'll be ready." And, just like that, she had another date with Drake Duncan.

And just to be sure she wasn't dreaming, when she got to her car thirty-five minutes later, Meg pulled out the brochure Drake had given her. The Leaping Lions in Wisconsin. It hadn't been a dream at all.

She could hardly wait for Saturday afternoon.

DRAKE HAD NEVER SEEN Meg look more beautiful than she did when he picked her up on Saturday afternoon. As if to fit in with the exotic atmosphere of the show, she'd rolled her chestnut hair into a French roll, and to the side of the thick plait of hair she'd placed a gold clip with a crimson hibiscus of silk. Her hairpiece was a fitting complement to the flowery pattern of the form-fitting dress that hugged her curves and swirled in a soft, colourful cloud around her ankles. A short gold jacket and gold sandals completed her elegant attire and Drake could not have been more proud to have her by his side.

They got to the Continental Hotel, the venue for the show, with a good forty-minutes to spare, and used the time to admire the South African art on display in the lobby. They were browsing, when Drake was recognized by the show promoter, and invited backstage to meet the performers. Meg had seemed perturbed by the attention, but eventually she calmed, and even exchanged a few words with some of the dancers. Before they left, the promoter made them promise to drop by the after-show party.

As they headed for their reserved seats, Meg raised an eyebrow. "A party, huh? I hope you can dance."

Drake gave her a rueful grin. "Not very well, I'm afraid. But maybe I'll pick up a few moves from tonight's show." And what a show it was. After a spectacular performance with dancers dressed in elaborate costumes in vibrant colours, and dances which seemed more like acrobatic feats, Drake and Meg left the hotel's grand ballroom in a daze.

"So, are you glad you came?" Drake asked, although he could already guess what her answer would be.

"Am I ever!"

He stared down at her face, wide-eyed and radiant, and he knew he had done the right thing in asking her out for the show. She looked like she hadn't had this sort of entertainment in a long while. He opened his mouth to tell her how beautiful she looked, when there was a shout, and he turned to see Mr. Promoter heading toward them. Crap. He'd been hoping to avoid the man.

But when their garrulous host reminded them of the party, Meg looked so eager that Drake didn't have the heart to say they were leaving. Another thirty or forty minutes wouldn't kill them, he guessed.

The anticipated thirty or forty minutes turned into almost two hours. The South African dancers and their man- agers were just as entertaining off stage as on. They insisted on teaching their guests some of their dance moves and then, before Meg and Drake knew what was happening, they found themselves in the middle of a Congo line. By the time they were able to escape, it was almost midnight.

As they walked back to the hotel lobby, Drake took her hand. "I'm sorry I kept you out so late. You must be exhaust-

ed."

"Me?" Her eyebrow shot up. "It's you, I'm worried about. How are you going to manage, making that long drive back

to Chicago? We won't get in till two in the morning." "Don't worry. I'm wide awake. I can make it." She bit her lip. "I don't know..."

"Hey," he said gently, "we can stay here, if you like." At her doubtful look, he said, "I think my credit is good at this place."

That made her smile. "I should think so."

"So, come on," he said, "let's get ourselves booked in. We can head back early tomorrow morning."

That night, just a few strokes before midnight, Drake walked Meg to the door of her hotel room. When she turned her face up to his, he could see the shadows of sleep clouding her eyes. "Good night, Meg," he said softly, and then, giving in to the urge, he pulled her into his arms.

She did not resist. She melted against him, her soft breasts pressing against his chest, and he yielded to the temptation of those lips that had been tormenting him all night. He bent his head and took possession of her mouth, groaning as she opened to him. He wrapped his arms around her, crushing her to his chest, then he kissed her until she clung to him as if she had no more strength left.

Finally, as much as he wanted more, he let his arms slide down and away, and then he stepped back. Her lips slightly swollen from the kiss, she was breathing heavily, gazing up at him from heavy-lidded eyes as she leaned back against the door. Was there any sight as sexy as a woman who'd just been thoroughly kissed? God knew, he wanted her more tonight than he ever had before. But no, he had to stay cool. He could not afford to rush and spoil everything.

"Goodnight, Meg," he whispered again, his voice hoarse this time.

"Goodnight, Drake," she whispered back and then, with an air of resignation, she turned and pushed her key card into the door. "I'll see you in the morning," she said softly, then turned the handle and went into her room, closing the door behind her.

Drake stared at the solid wooden panel of the door and cursed this barrier that stood between him and the woman he desired. He wanted to take her in his arms and make sweet love to her, but he could not. Slowly, he turned and walked to the elevator, then took it to the penthouse floor of the hotel where a suite had been prepared for him. This was where he wanted her, her body writhing under his, in an ultra-soft king-sized bed into which their bodies would melt. But it was not to be. Not tonight, anyway. He would have to do his best to take his mind off Meg.

Somehow, he had to cool down. Drake stripped and dropped his clothes on the bed, then walked, naked, to the bathroom. After brushing, he went to the shower and turned the water on. There, he stood under the stream as it cleansed his body and cleared his mind, making him alert again.

He threw on the luxurious robe the hotel had provided and walked back to the living room, where he flung himself onto the sofa. From where he sat, he had the perfect view of the suite's telephone. He stared at it. God, he wanted to call Meg. Even if nothing else came of it, he needed to hear her voice.

Just as he was reaching for the phone, it began to ring.

WITH PALMS GONE DAMP with her nervousness, Meg clutched the phone receiver and held it close to her ear. Had he already gone to bed? Would he think she was crazy to be calling him at this hour of the night? And what if he did answer the phone? Then what?

She bit her lip. She hadn't thought that far ahead. All she knew was that she didn't want the night to end. Even if all they did was talk, she just had to hear his voice. After she'd gone inside her hotel room, Meg had done the usual 'get-ready-for-bed' things – showered, brushed her teeth, brushed her hair till it fell in soft waves around her shoulders. Then, dressed in the hotel's terry robe, she'd climbed into bed to wait for sleep to claim her. No such luck. She'd tossed and rolled in the bed for almost half an hour before finally giving up. There was no way she was going to sleep tonight, not without talking to Drake one more time.

Truth be told, talk wasn't the only thing she wanted. In fact, it was sort of low on her priority list just then. There were so many other things, things that made her body shiver, just thinking about them.

But talking was a good way to start, so after minutes of hand wringing and deep breathing, she'd gathered her courage about her, picked up the phone and dialed.

Drake picked up on the first ring. "Hello."

His voice was deep and mellow, not like he'd been sleeping at all. Had he lain there, tossing and tortured as she had? "Hi, Drake," she said, her voice soft and hesitant. "I hope I didn't wake you."

"Not at all. I was just about to call you." "You...were?" Meg's heart skipped at his words.

"Yes, I was...thinking about you." There was a pause, then she heard him sigh. "I want you, Meg, so badly it hurts.

Can I see you tonight?"
Meg's breath caught in her throat. Had he really come out and asked that question? She hadn't expected that. Now what should she say?

"Yes." The word escaped her lips in a soft, breathless whisper. Her hand flew to her mouth and her heart began to pound faster. There. She'd said it. And now there was no turning back.

"I'll be down in a sec." "W...wait."

But he'd already hung up. Holy cow. Drake was on his way down to her hotel room and he was expecting sex. More hand wringing, palms growing even more moist. Could she handle it? Maybe she should call him back. But no, he'd probably already left the room.

She rested the phone receiver in its cradle and slid off the bed. Smoothing her damp palms down her hips, she dried them on the terry robe. Good heavens, was she ready for this? Maybe she should tell him no, that she'd made a mistake. Maybe she should-

There was a knock at the door and Meg started. He was here. Already? No more time for maybes. She took a deep breath and went to open the door.

Drake was standing in the doorway and as he looked down at her, his hair still damp from a recent shower, his eyes burned with a fierceness she had never seen before.

She stepped back, not saying a word. She didn't need to. She knew what she wanted, and the look in his eyes left her in no doubt as to what he wanted. This was going to happen.

He stepped into the room, closing the door behind him, and only then, did she realize that he was barefoot. Had he been in that much of a hurry?

Then, there was no more time for questions, no more time to think, because he reached for her, pulling her into his arms with a force that knocked the air from her lungs. His arm circled her back, locking her body to his, and then his hands went up, fingers sliding through her hair, to cup the back of her head and hold her at his mercy.

And then his mouth came down on hers, sensual and strong, subduing her with a kiss that drove all thought from her mind.

When he'd kissed her till her bones melted, leaving her soft and pliable in his arms, he bent to lift her and carry her over to the king-sized bed where he laid her on the pillows. Then, hands moving urgently, he pulled the knot in her sash and opened her robe, leaving her blushing and bare to his gaze.

He groaned, and as she moved her hands to cover her nakedness, he caught them, trapping her wrists against the bed, drinking his fill of the sight of her.

Holy heavens. No one had ever looked at her like that before. In his eyes, was a burning hunger that made her heart jerk in anticipation and just a hint of fear. She hadn't done this in so long. Would he be gentle?

He dipped his head, and in that move, he wiped the question from her mind because his lips, so masterful and firm, were now on her right breast, sucking, drawing its pink tip deep into his mouth. He played with that nipple, teasing and torturing, till she gasped in delight and arched her back, wanting even more.

To her relief, he obliged. Drake's urgent need seemed to match her own, because he released her breast, but just long enough to raise her up and pull the robe away from her body. He tossed it to the floor. Then, he was shedding his own clothes, swift fingers making fast work of the buttons on his shirt. In seconds he had it off, and threw it on the floor.

Meg's eyes widened and her mouth went dry. Holy Christ. She'd never been one to swear but, my goodness, did they build them this beautiful anymore? He was toned like a weapon of female destruction, the muscles cut in all the right places, the body tanned to perfection. She'd thought this man was a typical business executive with the body of someone who lived a sedentary lifestyle. But no, this man in front of her had the body of a professional athlete. He was like a well-honed machine, far advanced from what she'd seen ten years before.

But she should have known. When he'd pulled her close, he'd practically crushed her against a body that felt like rock. Now, she knew why. He was solid muscle. She hadn't quite finished admiring his upper body, when his hands fell to his trousers, and he began unbuckling his belt. She wanted to look away, she really did, but like a deer caught in headlights, all she could do was freeze. And hold her breath.

Then, in one smooth move, trousers and boxer shorts were sliding down firm, muscled legs, on their way to his feet. He stepped out of them then he straightened, moving so quickly she had no time to advert her eyes. But then, why should she? As nervous as she was, she was still enjoying the view.

Her eyes fell on the strength of his manhood as it stood rigid in its bed of soft, pale hair. His arousal was obvious in the throbbing of his member and the almost angry hue of its tip.

Meg swallowed hard.

She didn't have to do anything else, because Drake moved immediately to the bed and reached out to pull her into his embrace. He kissed her long and deep, her breasts crushed against his chest, his heart pounding like he'd just done a hundred-meter sprint.

When he released her, it was to press her back into the pillows, then he was kissing her neck, her breasts, sliding his lips down, down till he was licking her navel, teasing her with light flicks of his tongue, till she moaned.

What was he doing to her? Did he know he was driving her crazy? His tongue was turning her insides to liquid and, holy Mary, she was growing oh, so wet.

Meg sucked in her breath and reached for him. "Please," she whispered. "Please, Drake," she begged. "Now." The word was almost a sob. "I want you so much."

Immediately, he slid away from her off the bed. He reached down to where he had dropped his trousers and pulled his wallet out of his pocket. He dug around for about seven seconds and then a look of consternation crossed his face. Then, to Meg's dismay, his face fell in obvious disappointment.

She raised up off the pillow. "What? No condom?"

He put his hand to his forehead and groaned. "No condoms." With a look of disgust, he dropped the wallet on top of his trousers.

"But...how come?"

Drake drew in his breath and let it out again. Then, still looking like he could kick himself, he walked back to the bed and, with a heavy sigh, he lay down beside her. He gathered her into his arms and stroked her hair.

"I don't know if I should admit this, but I haven't done this in a while." He gave her crooked smile. "I bought a brand new pack a week ago and put it in my medicine chest at home. This morning I went into the bathroom specifically to put it into my wallet, when the phone rang and I went to get it. I completely forgot to go back and get the darned thing." He gave an exaggerated sigh. "Now, I remember."

She groaned and turned her face into his shoulder.

"I know, honey," he said softly, as he stroked her arm. "I know, but there's nothing we can do about it right now. There's no way the hotel gift and sundries shop would be open at almost one o'clock in the morning, and stuck out here in the boonies, it's not like we'll find any store near here that's open at this hour."

Meg groaned again, and this time she gave him a little bite on the shoulder. He jumped. "Hey, what was that for?"

"That's for leading me on and then torturing me." "I'm sorry," he said sadly. "I guess I deserve that."

For a moment, they lay there in each other's arms, then Meg spoke. "You know," she said softly, "We could still do it."

The hand that was stroking her shoulder came to a standstill. Drake looked down at her. "Are you sure you want to do that?"

"Well," she said, then paused. How to put this? "It's a bit embarrassing, but I'll tell you anyway. I...started taking the pill about a month ago."

She could feel her face turning red. *Please don't let him ask me why.*

He tilted his head to one side. "Really?"

"Yes," she said quietly, then seeing that she was the one who had brought up the topic, she decided to be brave. "Yes, I did, so we have nothing to worry about where pregnancy is concerned. And as for that other thing," she bit her lip then pressed on, "I haven't been with anyone since I lost my husband, and I've done several physicals since then." Her speech over, she peeked up at him. "What about you?"

A look of relief passed over his face. "Coincidentally, I did a physical just last month when I was upgrading my insurance plan. I got a clean bill of health." Then he gave her a thoughtful look. "But I don't have anything to prove that, Meg, not here. This is going to come down to trust. Do you trust me enough to let me make love to you...without protection?"

Meg looked up at him, and in her heart she had no doubt what her answer would be. "I trust you, Drake. And if you trust me, I want you to make love to me."

She could see that he needed no further encouragement. A smile broke across his face, and he leaned down to steal a kiss from her lips. Then, he raised himself up and, with a firm hand, he pressed her back into the pillows. To her delight, he continued where he'd left off, teasing and tickling her with soft kisses, making her body tingle with desire.

And then, when she thought she would burst with wanting him, he covered her body with his and she wrapped her legs around his lean hips and clung to him, her breath coming in pants. He aligned his body with hers and sank deep into her core.

"Drake," she gasped. "Oh, God, Drake." It was like she'd been waiting for this moment forever. Now, their bodies were one.

He let seconds pass, allowing her body to get used to his presence, and then he was moving, slowly and gently at first, then faster, until he was thrusting into her, riding a wave of passion, taking her with him over the crest where he exploded inside her as her inner core pulsated around him, sending sparks shooting to every inch of her body.

It took a long time for their panting gasps to slow to deep breaths and then to the normal rhythm of breathing. Only then, when their bodies had floated down from that pinnacle and the tension had dissolved, did they let each other go and fall back into the pillows.

"Oh, God, Meg," Drake breathed, "I've waited for this for so long, and it was worth every minute of the wait." She smiled, and as his chest rose and fell, she reached out to rest a hand on him. "For me, too, Drake. For me, too."

And as she lay in the bed beside him, Meg had no regrets; although there was still that little question in the back of her mind – where would they go from here?

CHAPTER NINE

"Liar, liar, pants on fire."

"Jessie." Meg's voice was stern. "Not nice, young lady. Now, go over and apologize."

Jessie's face fell, but she walked slowly over to the swing and regarded her classmate with a frown and a pout. "I'm sorry, Patrick." Then, with a whirl of her skirt she turned and headed back toward her mother.

Not a very gracious apology but one Meg would have to let slide right now. Just that week, she'd signed Jessie up for private piano lessons, and today was the first class. If they didn't move quickly, thewould be late. And for a class that lasted only half an hour they definitely couldn't afford to be late.

They made it to the class with five minutes to spare, thank goodness. While Jessie went to music room number three to plunk away at the piano, Meg settled herself in the most comfortable seat in the parents' waiting area, a big fat arm- chair, and pulled out her smartphone. She hadn't finished that romance novel she'd started so long ago. Right now, at least she could squeeze in the half hour Jessie's piano lesson would last.

For the last three weeks, she'd been working hard on Drake's project, determined to finish within the deadline she'd set herself. The contract said up to six months, but she wanted to prove to herself that she could do it in four. And besides, she didn't want to prolong her professional relationship with Drake. She was dying to make love to him again, but they'd both agreed that they should postpone any further intimate contact until they could openly start seeing each other. Before that could happen, the project would have to end. And the wait was killing her...or at least it felt like it. Thank goodness she was on the last lap. She'd already submitted her second draft and was now doing the final pass before presenting Drake with the official manuscript.

Yes, for the good of her sanity, this project would have to wrap up very soon. Because, how could you concentrate on something so mundane as a business memoir, when your breath caught in your throat every time those gorgeous gray eyes rested on you? And how could you take notes, when all you wanted to do was flick the pen away and reach over and slide your fingers through that thick, dark-blond hair? And how in heaven's name could you act cool and collected when the secretary came in to offer you tea, when all you wanted was to shove her boss back onto the sofa and kiss him till he begged for mercy?

Meg shook her head, bringing herself back to the present. She glanced at the clock. Jessie's half hour was almost up, and she hadn't read past the page she'd started on. It looked like she was destined never to finish this novel. Oh, well...

The following week, there was a stall in Meg's plan. She and Drake were to have had a final meeting before she prepared her complete package – hard and soft copies of the memoir, and a return of the tape recordings and notes. Where and when it was published, was up to Drake. Once Meg submitted her package, she would be free.

She'd been counting on catching an April fifteen date, but it was not to be. Drake ended up having to leave for a week on business, delaying the project past her four-month mark. There was nothing to do but wait.

But that weekend, days before Drake was to return, Meg was at the department store shopping with Jessie, when a thought crossed her mind.

When was the last time she'd had her period?

Her heart jerked. She started digging in her bag for her pocket agenda and flipped immediately to the calendar at the back. She'd always been regular, had never been more than a day or two late. But now? She rubbed her forehead as she checked the days. *Dear Lord, let her be wrong.* Maybe it had come last month, and she'd been so busy she'd forgotten?

"Mommy, can I get this baby bubble bath? It smells like strawberries." Jessie held up a teddy bear shaped bottle, cutting into Meg's thoughts.

"Not now, Jessie." Meg ran her fingers along the little boxes on the page, counting the days. Then, she looked up and her eyes glazed over as she stared straight ahead. Holy goodness. Holy Jeez. She was late by all of sixteen days. How the heck had she missed that?

"Mommy, I'm hungry."

Jessie's plaintive wail brought Meg back to the present. Hands trembling, she returned the tiny book to her bag and took her daughter's hand. "I'm sorry, honey. Mommy...was just a little distracted. Let's go pay for our stuff and then we'll get something to eat."

"Okay, Mommy." Jessie looked up at her with huge eyes, almost as if she knew something had gone wrong.

And a lot had.

Because there was no way she could tell Drake Duncan he was going to be a daddy.

WHAT THE HELL WAS GOING on? This was the third message Drake had left on Meg's cell phone, and still she had not returned his call. Could she be out of town? He glanced at the clock on the nightstand. Eleven thirty-seven. No, he could not call again. Definitely not at this hour.

He'd been back in Chicago one day now, but it felt like a week, because he'd been in the same city with Meg a whole day and still had not seen her. She'd become so important in his life, that he would be with her every day, if he could.

He lay back in the pillows and folded his arms behind his head. He would just have to be patient. They had their final meeting scheduled for tomorrow, and feeling like a schoolboy with a crush, he could hardly wait.

But the next day ended up being one of the strangest of Drake's life. One o'clock finally came and Meg walked into his office looking elegant and composed as she always did. But this time, there was something different about her. She'd greeted him warmly, giving him a smile and a nod, but she seemed distant, even cool. It was as if that night they'd shared had never happened.

When she handed him his final package, he'd expected jubilation, maybe a celebration, but not this aloofness that had him frowning and practically scratching his head. Then, when she got up to leave and he walked her to the door as he'd done so many times before, she dropped her eyes and dipped her head, hiding her face from view, but not before he'd seen an expression that made him pause. She'd almost looked like she wanted to cry.

"Meg, are you all right?" The door he was holding was half open, but he refused to let her through. He needed answers.

It was only then, that she lifted her head and looked him in the eyes. "I'm fine," she said quietly, and then she smiled.

And, as beautiful as that smile was, it was tinged with a sadness that squeezed his heart.

But he could see that she didn't want to talk. Now was not the time. Somehow, although he didn't know in what way, he knew that he'd hurt her...again.

For today, he would leave things be and give her some space, but next time he saw her, he would expect answers.

50 JUDY ANGELO

It was December fifteen, and Meg had just learned that she was going to become a mother for the second time. But this situation was so different from the first. How could she tell Drake he was going to be a father, when she'd assured him she wouldn't get pregnant? I've been on the pill a month, she'd said, so everything will be fine. Drake had trusted her, and then she'd gone and messed things up by getting pregnant with his child.

What made it worse, he'd already been deceived by a woman who'd used pregnancy as her weapon of choice. And, she knew, that was exactly what he would think of her. To him, she would be nothing more than a seductress who he would probably think was after his money.

Meg sighed. She would have to tell him, of course. But not now. Not until she was strong enough to deal with the condemnation in his eyes and the reproach she knew would come. Until then, she would stay away from him for as long as she could.

TWO DAYS WAS ENOUGH space, right? It had been hard but, not wanting to crowd her, Drake had deliberately held back from calling Meg. But it was Saturday morning now, so she should be more relaxed, probably back to her normal self. He would take the chance.

Drake dialed Meg's home number and waited. Three rings, four rings, five rings. It was probably going to switch to the answering machine next. He was just about to hang up when he heard a click and then a tiny voice on the phone.

"Hello?"

"Hi, Jessie, it's Drake. How are you?"

"I'm fine, thank you," came the faint reply. "May I speak to your mommy, please?"

"Mommy can't come to the phone. She's not feelin' too good. She's in the bathroom bein' sick again."

"Being sick?" A feeling of alarm shot up Drake's spine. Something was wrong with Meg. That was why she'd been behaving strangely. Then, a thought came to him. Nausea. Jessie had said she was being sick. Holy...was Meg doing chemotherapy?

"Who's helping her, Jessie?" "I am. I took her a towel."
"I mean, is there another adult in the house?" "No, just Mommy."
"Okay, tell Meg...your mom...I'm coming right over."

Within half an hour of the phone call, Drake was at Meg's door. As soon as Jessie opened it, he stooped to her eye level and smiled. Not wanting to scare her, he said, "I'm here to help your mommy, Jessie. Can you take me to her, please?"

She nodded, and the worried look on her face began to disappear. She gave him a little smile, not her usual bright smile, but it was a start. She reached out and took his hand, then began to pull him into the house. He barely had time to push the front door shut behind him, before she was pulling him down the hallway and toward the stairs.

But as anxious as she was, she was still not moving fast enough for Drake. He lifted the little girl into his arms and took the stairs two at a time.

When they got to the landing, she pointed to the first door. "That's Mommy's room."

Drake set Jessie gently on her feet then stepped toward the door, which was slightly ajar. He gave a quick tap and was listening for Meg's response when Jessie bounded forward and flung the door open.

"Mommy, Drake's here," she yelled and ran toward the bed which was now visible to Drake as he stood in the doorway.

There, propped up on the pillows, was Meg. And although she gave him a brave smile, he could see she was exhausted. When Jessie ran up and bounced onto the bed she winced and put a hand to her forehead, in obvious discomfort. Immediately, he went to her, the icy fingers of fear encircling his heart.

Oh, God, please don't let it be what I think it is.

As he went to stand by the bed, Drake saw how flushed Meg was, but while her face was pink ,there was a paleness to her lips that was not normal for her. Those lips were the first things he'd admired about her;; full and ruby red. Now all that color was gone. The dark shadows around her eyes told him she hadn't been sleeping well.

"Meg," he said, his voice sharp with reproach, "why didn't you call me? Why are you here, sick and all alone?" He leaned toward her. "I would have come. You know that."

"I'm fine, Drake. It's no big deal." But her tired eyes made a lie of what she'd just said.

"No, it's not fine. You're not fine." He folded his arms across his chest. "I'm disappointed in you, Meg." She'd looked sick before, but now, she also looked defiant. "Disappointed about what?"

"That you didn't feel that you could trust me enough with your secret." She gasped. "What secret?"

He glanced over at Jessie, who wasn't paying too much attention to their conversation. She was playing with her doll and seemed absorbed in that for the moment.

He cleared his throat. "May I talk to you in private, Meg?"

She stared up at him, her eyes full of suspicion. Then, never taking her eyes off him, she said, "Jessie, honey, can you go down and get me a glass of water, please?"

"Okay, Mommy." The child hopped off the bed and ran toward the door.

As soon as she was through it, Drake turned his attention back to Meg. "I...didn't want to ask this in front of Jessie but I have to know . Meg, please be honest with me. Are you on chemo?"

"Chemo?" Her eyes widened in obvious shock as she said the words.

"Yes." His shoulders slumped and he shoved his hands deep into his pockets. He shook his head. There was no gentle way to say this. "Do you have cancer?"

"Cancer?" Her voice came out indignant and strong, not what he'd expected. "Why would you ask such a thing?" He frowned, confused. "The nausea, being sick in the bathroom. Jessie told me about it and I thought-"

"Well, you thought wrong." She was glaring at him now. "But...what's wrong, then. Was it something you ate?"

"No, Drake, it wasn't something I ate." Her voice was exasperated now. Then, she fixed him with a withering look. "You hear that I'm nauseous and sick to my stomach and the first thing that comes to your mind is cancer?"

Nauseous. Sick to her stomach. Drake's jaw went slack, and his brows shot up as he stared at Meg. "Are you...pregnant?"

She gave him a look that said, "Finally, you idiot," then she pursed her lips and looked away, not seeming at all pleased. Didn't she want his baby?

But in the middle of that thought, realizing that Meg was, in fact cancer-free, relief washed over him. He'd never in his life been so happy to be wrong.

"Meg," he whispered, "you're expecting my child?" He had to hear it from her mouth. "Yes." Her voice was a mere whisper and the look she gave him was full of apprehension.

He stepped forward, his heart almost bursting with his love for her. "You know what this means, don't you?" Eyes huge in her distress, she shook her head slowly.

"It means, my dear Meg, that you will have to marry me."

She looked taken aback, her eyes huge in her face. "Marry me? You still want to marry me?"

"Now, more than ever," he said, and there was not an ounce of doubt in him. "I asked you to marry me months ago and I'm asking you again now. Will you marry me, Meg? I want you to be my wife. I want to be a father to my child." Then, as she still stared up at him, a look of disbelief on her face, he said, "And I want to be a father to Jessie as well. Will you let me?"

That got a reaction from Meg, not the romantic one he was expecting, where she flung her arms around his neck and cried, "I do, I do." She sat up in the bed and folded her arms across her chest. "So, you're not angry with me?" she demanded.

"Angry? I'm over the moon. Why would I be angry about the best thing that could ever happen to me?"

Still looking unconvinced, she cocked her head to one side. "So, you're not mad that I told you I wouldn't get pregnant because I was on the pill, and then still got pregnant anyway?"

Now, it was his turn to sound exasperated. "No, Meg, why should I?"

"But you told me about that woman who tried to use a pregnancy to trap you-"

"That was a made-up pregnancy, just something she came up with to get me down the aisle. But in your case," he sat on the bed and drew her into his arms, "I was the one trying to draw you to the altar." Then, he chuckled. "You silly woman, I already asked you to marry me, or did you forget? Could I want to marry you and then be upset that you're carrying my child? You don't understand, Meg. This is the happiest day of my life."

She turned her face up to his, searching his eyes. "Honest?"
"Cross my heart and hope to die."

At the words, the tension in her dissolved, and she relaxed against him. He used the opportunity to wrap his arms around her. Then, he put his lips close to her ear. "So," he whispered softly, "I'm asking my question yet again. My dearest Meg, will you marry me?"

She slid her arms around his waist and hugged him tight. "Yes," she said, and the word came out in a little sob. "Yes, I'll marry you, Drake Duncan. I've loved you for too long to let you go. I want to be your wife and the mother of your child."

He let out a deep sigh and leaned down to softly kiss her lips. "I'll go get Jessie," he said, with a smile filled with love. "Time to give her the good news."

And as he turned to get up off the bed, he saw little Jessie standing in the doorway, a glass of water in her hand. And she was beaming.

"Are you going to be my daddy?" she whispered, her eyes huge in her face.

Drake smiled at her. "If you'll have me," he said gently.

"Yes," Jessie said, with a little squeal. "Yes, please. That's what I want for Christmas. I want you to be my daddy."

"Then you shall have me, little one. Like you wanted, you 'll have a daddy for Christmas."

And as little Jessie ran into Drake's arms, he scooped her up and walked over to wrap Meg in that same warm embrace, the embrace of a newly-formed family, a family that would soon be spending many Christmases together.

For Drake, there could be no better Christmas gift than that.

EPILOGUE

The strains of 'I'll be home for Christmas' faded away and then Meg's all-time favorite came on, Bing Crosby's rendition of 'White Christmas'. He was the ultimate crooner, as far as she was concerned. This was her favorite time of year, and she just could not get enough of the Christmas carols.

In less than twenty-four hours, it would be Christmas Day, their second Christmas as a family, and she could hardly wait. With a sigh, she sank deeper into the rocking chair and as Bing Crosby crooned the words to the beloved carol she looked down into the angelic face of her infant son, Drake Duncan II.

He was the perfect gift, born three months earlier, a seven pounder. He was going to be tall like his father. She could see it in the length of his little legs. And he would be just as handsome. He was the most beautiful baby she had ever seen. Next to Jessie, of course.

"Can I hold him, Mommy?"

Meg looked up as her daughter walked into the sitting room, looking so serious and big-sisterly. At six years old, she now considered herself a big girl, and more than capable of caring for her baby brother. "I'll let you hold him," Meg said, "if you sit on that cushion on the floor and you stay very still. Can you do that?"

"Of course, Mommy. I know how to hold Drake. I've done it before."

Meg raised an eyebrow. "Oh? And when was that?"

"Daddy let me hold him when you were sleeping," she began, then she bit her lip, and her eyes grew round. "Are you mad?"

Meg gave her a soft smile as she settled onto the cushion. "No, Jessie, I'm not mad." She got out of the rocker and went to lay the baby gently across Jessie's lap. "But I do need to speak to your daddy. Where is he?"

"Right here, sweetheart." The deep voice ca me from the doorway and when she looked up, there stood her husband of seven months, looking so handsome in a black turtleneck sweater that showed off his muscled frame.

She raised an eyebrow. "And what happened to the Christmas tree sweater your mother sent?"

He grimaced. "Maybe tomorrow. Not sure I can stand the torture today." Then he smiled and opened his arms to her, and Meg walked into his embrace. He gave her a kiss on the forehead. "How's my girl doing?"

She sighed as she leaned into him. "Doing fine, now that your namesake is fed and asleep. I wonder if you were as ravenous when you were a baby?"

Drake chuckled. "You can ask my mom when she gets here tomorrow." He looked over at Jessie holding Baby Drake and smiled. "She's such a great big sister," he whispered so that only Meg could hear, "and the best daughter I could ever ask for."

Her heart swelling with love for him, Meg slid her arms around his waist and squeezed him tight. "And you're the best daddy I could ever want for Jessie and Drake."

With her head resting against him, Meg heard the rumble of laughter in Drake's chest. She lifted her face and peered up at him. "What's so funny?"

"I'm just remembering when Jessie told me last year that she wanted a daddy by December twenty-four. She'd wanted one as a special Christmas gift for you, she'd said. She got her wish, so I guess there really is a Santa Claus."

Meg sighed with contentment and laid her head back on his chest. "I guess there is," she said softly. "I couldn't have asked for a nicer gift."

And as she relaxed in Drake's embrace, her thoughts went back to Jessie's drawing of the family she'd wished for. She would have to remind her to do another one, now that baby made four.

This would be her first Christmas with her wonderful family of, not three, but four. *Thank you, Santa.*

54

56 JUDY ANGELO

Sneak Preview of the next in the series:

"Are you kidding me?"

THE BILLIONAIRE BROTHERHOOD SERIES

VOLUME 8

To Catch a Man (in 30 Days or Less) CHAPTER ONE

"Are you kidding me?"

Randolph Marshall shook his head. "I'm dead serious. You have until October twenty-three, or you forfeit fourteen million dollars."

"Fourteen million..." Indiana Lane's voice trailed off as she stared across the desk at the attorney. "No, you've got to be kidding me." She looked around the room. "I'm on 'Candid Camera', right? Or one of those other crazy prank TV shows?" She began to chuckle, as she turned to look back at him.

"Miss Lane, trust me. I do not have time for pranks." Exasperation dripped from each word. "I'm an old man with a bad heart. I don't play games. I tell it as it is. Do you understand me?"

Indie's smile began to fade as she stared back at the now frowning man. Okay, so he really was serious. He was shaking his graying head and looking at her like he wanted to give her a sharp rap on the knuckles. Ouch.

"Yes," she said, gripping the arms of the chair, "I understand you but...but he hardly even knew me."

Marshall looked unimpressed. "He seems to have known you well enough to want to make you a rich woman. Under certain conditions, of course."

"But...but..." She was spluttering again. *Come on, Indie, this is so not like you. You've negotiated with guerilla fighters and warlords and you're thrown upside down by this?* She drew in a slow, deep breath then got up and shoved her hands deep into her trouser pockets. Her brain worked better when she was standing.

"So let me get this straight. Based on the stipulations in my uncle's will I have to find a man in the next..." she frowned, thinking, "...thirty days, fall in love, and get married in order to inherit this fourteen million dollars?"

Randolph cocked a grizzly eyebrow. "Nobody said anything about falling in love."

"Well, I can't very well just run off and marry the next man I run into, can I? One would hope I'd at least feel some- thing for him...and he, for me." She stopped talking when she saw the attorney's expression. Was the man laughing at her?

"A real idealist, I see." His smile was broader than the Cheshire Cat's.

That got her riled up. "And who says I want his money, anyway?" The man was looking too smug, and it was pissing her off. Big time. "Money has never been the biggest thing in my life, Mr. Randolph Marshall. And neither has marriage. I can do without both of them-"

"Yes, Miss 'Save-The-World'. I know. And that's exactly why your uncle did what he did. Don't you worry. He filled me in on all the details."

Now, on top of pissing her off, he was confusing the heck out of her. "What details?"

"Remember that conversation you had with him right after your mother's funeral?" She frowned. "That was nine years ago."

"Yes," Randolph said, with a nod. "You were twenty-one years old, and you sat in the library, spouting off your idealistic philosophies to Samuel about not wanting to get married or have children. There are too many homeless kids in the world for you to even think of starting a family of your own. Isn't that what you said?"

Indie straightened to her full five-foot-nine-inch height and frowned at Marshall. What was he getting at? "Yeah, so what? I still think the same way."

Marshall nodded slowly. "Ah-ha. And that's what your uncle was afraid of." He leaned forward and propped his elbows on the desk. "You're going to be thirty years old in thirty days, Indiana. Thirty. Think of it. That old, and no man and no kids. No life, except for running off to the favelas of Brazil to save orphans or chopping through the bushes and jungles of Colombia to search out drug dealers selling girls as sex slaves. Where were you this time? Africa?"

"Haiti," she said, her tone sullen.

The lawyer heaved a sigh. "Haiti. And where next? Cambodia?" He shook his head. "Listen. Your uncle wants his bloodline to continue. He never had kids and you, his sister's child, are his only hope of that. He wants you to get cracking while your eggs are still viable."

"He what?" Indie almost burst out laughing. The audacity of the man. "He actually said that?"

"Yes, and more, but..." Marshall put his hand up, "you don't want to know." He leaned back in his chair and clasped his hands behind his head. "So, are you on board? Can I cross you off my list of things to do this month and consider this sealed and set?"

Indie could only shake her head in disbelief. Between the lawyer and her now dead uncle, she didn't know which one was battier. They'd probably both been smoking the same...prohibited substance.

"Now you listen to me, Mr. Marshall." She fixed him with a glare of defiance. "I have two things to say to you. Number one, I don't want a single dime of Uncle Sam's fourteen million dollars. I've gotten along quite well without his help and will continue to survive, I'm sure. And number two," she raised an eyebrow, "if he'd wanted me to be married, barefoot and pregnant by age thirty, he should have spoken a heck of a lot earlier than September twenty-three."

For a long moment, Marshall just stared at her, his lips pursed, then he nodded solemnly. "Well said, but let me implore you to think about it. You're so concerned about doing good in the world, do you know how much more you could do with fourteen million dollars?" He paused, as if to let that sink in. "And as for the timing, I think I know what happened." He glanced down, shifted a couple of papers, then picked up the will. He reached for his glasses, put them on, then peered at the document. "Yes," he said, with a sigh, "I was right. He miscalculated your age. When he updated this four years ago, he had you down as twenty-four years old, but you were actually twenty-five." He looked up at her, peering over the top of his glasses like an old owl. "I guess he was planning to tell you, but was biding his time, watching to see if things would work out. Probably thought he had at least a few more months before he had to tackle you on such a touchy subject." He shrugged. "Who was to know he'd have been taken out by a heart attack at age sixty-six?"

Marshall's speech had Indie staring at him in shock. She was so worked up, she didn't know what to say. Then, she snorted. "Yeah, right. He thought I was a year younger? Do you realize if he hadn't died when he did, I would have soon passed his stupid deadline for me? I'll be thirty in a month."

"Yeah, well." Marshall shrugged. "If he'd lived, he probably would have updated the will. The pity is, he never got a chance to realize or correct his miscalculation. And with him being dead, you're stuck with it."

"This is so stupid," Indie muttered, as she got up and began to pace the room. "Stupid, stupid."

"I know. But it is what it is. Fourteen million dollars or zilch. Your call." The lawyer began to slide the documents back into the case. "You know where to find me, Indiana. I leave everything in your hands. Just remember the date – October twenty-three, by midnight."

And with that, Indie knew she was being dismissed. The man had other clients to deal with, other more pressing business. He was probably checking the clock to make sure she didn't run over her portion of his 'billable hour' or what- ever it was lawyers called it.

And at the same time he was dismissing her, he'd thrown her normally well-ordered life into a whirlpool of indecision. Where in the world should she go from here? And if she did decide to fulfill Sam's condition, where the heck should she start looking for a man to marry...in thirty days?

STONE HUDSON SKIPPED channels, trying desperately to find a station with music that would keep him awake. The evening traffic was brutal, jamming up all the way from Oakville. He wouldn't make it to Burlington for another thirty minutes, at this rate. He heaved a sigh and surfed more channels.

He was one tired son-of-a-gun, up for the past twenty-two hours since leaving Johannesburg the day before. The valet had brought his car and he'd driven out of the Toronto Pearson Airport exactly thirty-eight minutes ago, but still he was only a little more than halfway home.

Stubborn brute that he was, he'd insisted on driving his Maserati home. Now, he could only shake his head in regret. This was one of those days when he should have let the chauffeur come and get him. Damn him for always having to be in control. He hated being in a vehicle where he wasn't the one behind the wheel, but that ultra-independent trait of his was certainly working against him this evening.

He shook his head and blinked to clear the cobwebs from his eyes, then stifled a yawn. He turned the radio up as loud as he could stand it, and turned the air conditioning up full blast. It was going to be rough going, trying to stay awake in traffic that was almost at a standstill.

Maroon five's 'One More Night' was pounding in his ears when traffic got unplugged and began to move. Finally. A slight smile crept across his lips. The images were so vivid now – home, a soothing bath, bed, sliding under the cool sheets, his head sinking into the soft pillows, closing his weary eyes-

Wham!

Stone's head jerked up and he slammed on the brake. What the-

He blinked. And then he groaned. He'd run into the back of an army-green Land Rover. Christ!

Cursing himself for being such a clutz, he began to pull over onto the soft shoulder. The Land Rover was pulling over, too. He groaned. Just what he needed. A rear-ending as a fitting close to his journey of almost twenty-four hours. He'd learned his lesson – no more pretending to be Superman on these long trips.

Stone grabbed his wallet off the front passenger's seat and slid out of the car. Reaching up to massage the back of his neck, he stifled another yawn. God, he was tired. He blinked to clear the gravel from his eyes, then walked over to meet the guy who was climbing out of the Land Rover.

A quick glance told Stone his Maserati hadn't suffered a scratch. The other vehicle was another matter. It now sported a smashed-in back bumper. He steeled himself for the swearing. This was going to be one pissed-off dude.

The other driver was coming toward him now, a slender kid of medium height with short black hair that glistened in the sun. Plaid shirt rolled up at the sleeves, jeans and Timberland boots, he must have been coming from work. *Sorry to spoil the end of your work day, kid.*

Stone glanced down and began digging his driver's license out of his wallet. When he looked up again, the kid was standing right in front of him, green eyes flashing, soft pink lips set in an angry pout.

Huh? Stone's gaze dropped to the plaid-covered chest and there, pert and pointing straight at him, was his confirmation. The dude was a girl.

"Hey, what's up with you, fella? Falling asleep at the wheel?"

Stone frowned. Kind of aggressive, wasn't she? It was when she got closer, that he saw that she wasn't so much a girl as she was a woman, probably in her late twenties, maybe about four or five years younger than he was. And she was tall. Well, for a woman. The top of her head was just shy of his earlobe and he was six-foot-three.

And her eyes, so like those of a cat, were practically cutting him to shreds. With her high cheekbones, long nose and tanned skin, she looked like a Native American princess. But it was those eyes, like green shards of glass fringed with incredibly long lashes, that had him staring like a dumbstruck fool.

"What? Cat got your tongue?"

It took that sarcastic remark to snap Stone out of his daze. He scowled. He wasn't used to being on the receiving end of such biting remarks, least of all from a woman. Most of the women he knew would be falling over themselves to impress him. At least, the ones who knew who he was.

He didn't bother to respond. He could see that this was a feisty one and he wasn't in the mood for a shouting match. Instead, he held out his driver's license. "Here's my information," he said, his voice all business. "You can make a note while I grab my insurance papers." When she didn't take the card from his hand, he rested it on the hood of his car then walked around to the passenger's side of the Maserati, where he flipped open the glove compartment and grabbed his documents.

When he went back to the front of his car, Miss Brave and Bold was bending over, examining the damage to her back bumper, giving him a pretty good view of her taut derriere. Nice.

As he got closer, she straightened. "Not too bad. The bang sounded a lot worse than it looks." She gave him a bold stare, then held out her driver's license to him. "Here. I'll go write your stuff down while you do mine." She dropped the card into his palm and stepped over to where he'd left his driver's license, her movements smooth and lithe, like an athlete's.

Stone stared after her, but she paid him no mind. Strange. His stares were known to set the ladies tittering. But not this one. It was obvious that she was not easily impressed or intimidated.

She picked up the card and stared at it for a couple of seconds. Then she lifted it closer to her face and a chuckle escaped her lips. Then it turned into an all-out laugh.

Stone scowled. It wasn't his best picture but, come on, it wasn't that bad. He stepped closer and stared at his driver's license in her long, lean fingers. "What's so funny?" he growled.

"Your...your name," she said, in between laughs. She turned her eyes on him and this time, instead of cutting anger, they were filled with dancing mirth. "Is your name really..." more laughter, "...Gladstone? You don't look like a Gladstone to me." And more laughter tumbled from her lips as she staggered back and leaned against the hood, clutching her chest in a fake laughter-induced heart attack.

His face grew as dark as his mood. The woman was laughing at him. "It's Stone," he said, his voice cold and hard. "Stone Hudson." No-one called him by his first name. Absolutely no-one. They knew better. Until this woman came along...

Still laughing, she nodded. "Okay, Gladstone...Stone, I got you." Then, still chuckling, she pushed up and off the hood and headed for her SUV, the card still in her hand.

Stone stayed where he was, still simmering, and as he watched her through the back glass, he saw her pick up a pen and pull a small notepad from the bag on the passenger's seat. She began to write. And she was still chuckling.

Stone glared at the back of her head, feeling like he could happily wring her neck, but of course, he could not. Frustrated, he growled deep in his throat, then looked down at the card in his hand. "Indiana Moon Lane", it read. And, like him, she had a Burlington address. Twenty-nine years old with a birthday coming up in a month. So, he was right. She was four years his junior. And, like most driver's licenses, the picture didn't do her any justice. In the photo, her hair was much longer, falling in a black curtain to her shoulders and her face looked thin. But those eyes could never be hidden. They jumped out at you, sharp as daggers, and that determined set of her mouth told anyone looking on, that she was a force to be reckoned with.

"Got everything you need?"

He looked up to see her standing beside him. How the heck had she done that? He hadn't heard a sound, but there she was, right by his elbow.

"Just a sec." He reached through the window of his car and grabbed the novel he'd bought in the airport. Quickly, he copied her particulars into the back of the book, and when she handed him her insurance papers, he recorded that information as well. He turned around to hand them back to her, but she had her back to him, her cell phone positioned as she took photos of her car.

"For the record," she said, and gave him a smile that wasn't mocking or sarcastic, but wide and genuine and beautiful, a smile that so transformed her face that he couldn't help but stare. Again.

For a moment, they both stood there – he, staring at her and she, smiling at him. She almost looked like she wanted to say something else, probably even strike up a real conversation, nothing to do with cars or accidents. He certainly did. But then, just as he was about to speak, she took the papers from him then stepped back and lifted her hand in a little wave. "Well, I've got to run," she said. "Got things to do and people to see. In fact," she glanced away and a look of concern flitted across her face, "I'd better get cracking on my next assignment, as crazy as it is."

Crazy assignment? That piqued his interest, but he got no chance to ask questions. She was already walking back to her SUV.

Indiana Moon Lane slid into the driver's seat, started the vehicle, and without a backward glance, she merged into the slow-moving traffic and was gone.

Stone, half bewildered, half intrigued, stared after her. This woman, so fearless and direct, was a world apart from the hothouse flowers he was used to. In fact, she looked like she'd be happier on the wide open plains of the wild west or the jungles of South America than stuck in the middle of traffic on a Canadian highway.

Then a thought came to him, a crazy thought, but he couldn't shake it. What if she was the one he'd been looking for all along?

To read more about Indiana and Stone, get your copy of 'To Catch a Man (In 30 Days or Less)' from your favourite online retailer.

62 THE BILLIONAIRE BROTHERHOOD
Volume 1 - Tamed by the Billionaire
Volume 2 - Maid in the USA
Volume 3 - Billionaire's Island Bride
Volume 4 - Dangerous Deception
Volume 5 - To Tame a Tycoon
Volume 6 - Sweet Seduction
Volume 7 - Daddy by December
Volume 8 - To Catch a Man (in 30 Days or Less)
Volume 9 – Bedding her Billionaire Boss
Volume 10 - Her Indecent Proposal
Volume 11 - So Much Trouble When She Walked In
Volume 12 – Married by Midnight

THE BILLIONAIRE BROTHERS KENT
Book 1 - The Billionaire Next Door
Book 2 - Babies for the Billionaire
Book 3 - Billionaire's Blackmail Bride
Book 4 - Bossing the Billionaire

THE CASTILLOS
Book 1 - Beauty and the Beastly Billionaire
Book 2 – Training the Tycoon
Book 3 – The Mogul's Maiden Mistress
Book 4 – Eva and the Extreme Executive

HOLIDAY EDITIONS
Rome for the Holidays (Novella)
Rome for Always (Novel)

The NAUGHTY AND NICE Series
Volume 1 - **Naughty by Nature**

COMEDY, CONFLICT & ROMANCE Series
Book 1 - Taming the Fury
Book 2 - Outwitting the Wolf
Book 3 - Romancing Malone
THE BILLIONAIRE BACHELORETTES OF BEL-AIR
Book 1 -In Bed with the Enemy
NOVELLAS
The Billionaire's Bold Bet
Tamed by the Billionaire - The Sequel
COLLABORATIONS
A is for Arrangement – Eden Adams
INTERNATIONAL
SPA - Domado por el Multimillionario
FRE - La Milliardaire Apprivoisee
SPA - Romance de la Criada en los EU
FRE - En Amour avec la Femme de Chambre
GER - Vom Milliardar Gezahmt
SPA - La Novia Cautiva del Multimillionario
SPA - Engano Peligroso
JAP - For titles in Japanese, contact Tuttle Mori Agency,
Tokyo
NONFICTION
How to Write a Romance Novel
COLLECTIONS
THE BILLIONAIRE BROTHERHOOD, Coll. I - Vols. 1
- 4

THE BILLIONAIRE BROTHERHOOD, Coll. II - Vols. 5 - 8

THE BILLIONAIRE BROTHERHOOD, Coll. III - Vols. 9 - 12

BILLIONAIRE BROS. KENT - Books 1 - 4

THE BILLIONAIRE BROTHERHOOD DOUBLE COLLECTION - Vols. 1 - 8

THE BILLIONAIRE BROTHERHOOD MEGA-COLLECTION - Vols. 1 - 12

THE BILLIONAIRE BROTHERS KENT - Vols. 1 - 4

THE CASTILLOS - Vols. 1 - 4

COMEDY, CONFLICT & ROMANCE - Vols. 1 - 3

HOME for the HOLIDAYS - Vols. 1 - 3

Author contact:
judyangeloauthor@gmail.com

This book is a work of fiction. The names, characters, places, and incidents are products of the writer's imagination or have been used fictitiously. Any resemblance to persons, living or dead, is entirely coincidental.

Author contact: judyangeloauthor@gmail.com

Don't miss out!

Visit the website below and you can sign up to receive emails whenever JUDY ANGELO publishes a new book. There's no charge and no obligation.

https://books2read.com/r/B-A-WPD-MFN

BOOKS 2 READ

Connecting independent readers to independent writers.

Did you love *Daddy by December*? Then you should read *Rome for the Holidays*[1] by JUDY ANGELO!

Talk about sexy as sin...

Arie Angelis is floored when she lays eyes on the handsome hunk seated at the head table at the holiday event she's catering. She literally can't take her eyes off him. She's always prided herself on being the consummate professional, but not this time. But, attracted or not, when she finds out who he is she realizes he's way out of her reach. But you can't stop a girl from dreaming...

Rome Milano is used to getting what he wants but when he meets the hot and heavenly Arie Angelis he learns that he can't always have his way. He's used to calling the shots but, if the lady has her way, not this time...

---

1. https://books2read.com/u/mlKRwY

2. https://books2read.com/u/mlKRwY

Also by JUDY ANGELO

Bad Boy Billionaires - Where Are They Now?
Tamed by the Billionaire - The Sequel

Billionaire Bachelorettes of Bel-Air
In Bed with the Enemy

KNOWLEDGE in a NUTSHELL
How to Write a Romance Novel

MADE FOR THE MOVIES Fantasy Romance
Trading Spaces
Back from the Future

Multimillonarios Machos
Domado por el Multimillionario, Bilingual Version

The BAD BOY BILLIONAIRES Series
To Tame a Tycoon
Sweet Seduction
Daddy by December
To Catch a Man (in 30 Days or Less)
Bedding Her Billionaire Boss
Her Indecent Proposal
So Much Trouble When She Walked In
Married by Midnight
Bad Boy Billionaires - Collection II, Vols. 5 - 8
Bad Boy Billionaires Collection III, Vols. 9 - 12
Bad Boy Billionaires Mega-Collection Vols 1 - 12

THE BILLIONAIRE BROTHERHOOD
Tamed by the Billionaire (Roman's Story)
Maid in the USA (Pierce's Story)
Billionaire's Island Bride (Dare's Story)
Dangerous Deception (Storm's Story)
The Billionaire Brotherhood Collection I, Vols. 1 - 4
Bad Boy Billionaires Double Collection, Vols. 1 - 8

The Billionaire Brothers Kent
The Billionaire Next Door
Babies for the Billionaire
Billionaire's Blackmail Bride
Bossing the Billionaire
The Billionaire Brothers Kent

The BILLIONAIRE HOLIDAY Series
Rome for the Holidays
Rome for Always
Home for the Holidays

The Castillos
Beauty and the Beastly Billionaire
Training the Tycoon
The Mogul's Maiden Mistress
Eva and the Extreme Executive
The Castillos - The Collection

The Comedy, Conflict and Romance Series
Taming the Fury
Outwitting the Wolf
Romancing Malone
Comedy, Confict & Romance - The Collection

The Naughty and Nice Series
Naughty by Nature

Standalone
The Billionaire's Bold Bet

Lightning Source UK Ltd.
Milton Keynes UK
UKHW010821250223
417646UK00004B/453

9 798201 523800